Not Christmas Without You

NOT CHRISTMAS WITHOUT YOU

A Love on Chance Avenue Romance

JANE PORTER

TULE
PUBLISHING

DEDICATION

Dedicated to my readers everywhere.
I write each and every book for you!

With special thanks to my JP Street Team and my Jane Porter Facebook group for being so supportive always, as well as grateful thanks and love to Lee Hyat, Elisabeth Ringvard, Shari Bartholomew, Michelle Roark, Heidi Pergolski, and Jerilynn Moselle for giving me wonderful feedback on this story in particular!

And last but not least, thank you to Meghan Farrell Fuhrmann, for your help. I am beyond grateful and I wouldn't have a Christmas story every year if it wasn't for you!

CHAPTER ONE

I T WASN'T THE worst breakup in history.

Charity Wright knew that on the spectrum of heartbreaks, hers was mild. It was the sort of thing that someone might say "I have a touch of the flu," except hers was a touch of heartbreak. Not so devastating that the holidays would be completely ruined but dispiriting, for sure. She secretly suspected that she might be getting too old to believe that happy-ever-afters could exist. And yet, she wasn't a good pessimist. She preferred to see the glass as half-full, but on the inside she was increasingly worried. Was something wrong with her?

Why couldn't she meet "the one"? Or, had she met the one—her thoughts immediately went to her first love, Joe Wyatt, before shying away—and she'd blown her only opportunity for happy-ever-after? Maybe soul mates didn't exist. Maybe there wouldn't be a Mr. Right for her, never mind a Mr. Perfect.

Her younger sister, Amanda, said Charity hadn't found Mr. Right because Charity's standards weren't high enough—at least not since Joe, and he was years ago.

Older-sister Jenny said it was because all those romance novels Charity had read growing up had poisoned her brain, making her think that love was easy and fun. Obviously Jenny had never read a romance novel, because in romance, love was not easy *or* fun. Love was a battlefield, with a little nod to the great 80s' singer, Pat Benatar.

This was why Charity needed a break from men and dating. She was just too banged up. A little too bruised. Charity was usually a never-ending well of hope, but at the moment, her hope was running dry. Which was why she kept thinking about Tricia's offer to attend the travel agent familiarization trip in Wyoming in Tricia's place.

It'd be a chance to get away from Marietta, a chance to have a break from the real estate office—as she unfortunately worked with her ex, the double-timing Greg—and a chance to go somewhere she'd never been. The Tetons were only a five-hour drive from Marietta, but she'd never been.

Growing up, the Wright sisters hadn't traveled much because the family didn't have the means to travel, never mind manage rent and food. But Charity was thirty now, and this travel agent familiarization would get her there, and even better, it was free. A four-night, five-day all-expense paid trip to a little ski resort in Wyoming. Would it be so wrong to go?

Was it so awful to pretend to be Tricia Thorpe instead of Charity Wright?

It wasn't as if Tricia was a stranger. Tricia had been a

close friend since they were girls, and Tricia's brother married Charity's sister, Jenny, making them family. And since Tricia couldn't go on the trip due to a work conflict, and the Little Teton ski resort really wanted Marietta Travel to participate, why couldn't Charity represent Marietta Travel?

It wasn't as if Charity knew nothing about the travel agency. She'd worked for them one summer when they were shorthanded and she was in between jobs. True, she hadn't actually booked travel, but she'd filed brochures and printed travel itineraries and assisted the agents with their research. She actually quite liked the job. She'd hoped they would hire her and train her, but they had wanted someone with experience, someone who already knew how to use the computer software and had a client base. That's how Charity had ended up working for Sam Melk at Melk Realty, and then how she met Greg, who'd been hired a year after she started there. They were no longer dating, but Greg remained a problem, making little digs, constantly goading her. Charity shouldn't have ever dated him in the first place, but what was done was done. All she could do was move forward.

A trip to Wyoming sounded like the perfect break, a most welcome break. Provided she didn't have to ski—of course she'd been skiing at Bridger Bowl, just outside of Bozeman and she'd also done a little bit of skiing at Big Sky—but she was still quite an intermediate skier, and wasn't cut out for black diamond anything.

Tricia had said no skiing was required. Tricia said Charity simply needed to soak up all the information and report back, and if there was anything Charity did well, it was taking notes.

Charity shut down her computer, walked through Melk Realty turning off printers and lights, adjusting the thermostat for the night, before locking the door on the office and making her way two blocks south on Main Street to Marietta Travel.

Outside, festive white lights framed the windows and green garland wrapped around the light posts lining the street. The decorations on Main Street were familiar and beloved, and while Charity cherished her life in Marietta, there were disadvantages to living in a small town. She knew everyone, and everyone knew her, which also meant they knew when her romantic life derailed.

Marietta Travel still blazed with light and, peeking through the front window painted with a huge blue globe, topped with a jaunty red ribbon and the words *The World is Yours* in a gorgeous font, Charity spotted Tricia still at her desk in the glassed-in office at the very back.

Charity gave the painted window a quick critical study before trying the door. The paint was holding up. Good. She'd worried it might crack with the cold but it looked perfect still. No one but Tricia knew Charity had painted the window when Tricia's usual sign painter tripped on his own icy sidewalk and broke his wrist, preventing him from doing the job. Tricia knew that Charity was forever sketching clothes, and asked Charity if she'd be willing to decorate their window for the Marietta Stroll, and Charity hadn't been able to turn down the chance to make a little extra money on the side. With both of her parents now retired, money in her family was always tight.

Charity stuck her head inside the front door and called to Tricia, "Hey, Trish, am I interrupting?"

Tricia left her desk and waved her in. "Just wrapping up a few things. Come on back."

"Anything I can help with?"

"Nope, just organizing itineraries to go out to customers tomorrow." Tricia gave her a hopeful look. "Have you decided about the Little Teton familiarization trip?"

"I think I want to do it."

"Good! It should be fun. Most of the agents will probably be older, but there might be a few other young ones."

"I don't care about that. I'd love to be able to help you. You're always looking out for me."

"Well, it would help us. The owners really want Marietta Travel there, aware that we have some clients with deep pockets, and you know our clientele. You know what people here are looking for when they say they want a great weekend getaway, or a cool, but affordable ski trip."

"I do think it'd be fun to learn something new. I promise to take extensive notes."

"I know you will. That's why I'm encouraging you to go. You go be our ears and eyes, report back if Little Teton is the new place for us to recommend." Tricia gave her a sly look. "It also means you'd miss the Stroll this weekend, and we all know Greg is going to parade his Miss Livingston around all weekend. Do you really want to be there to see that?"

"*No.*" That alone made Charity shudder. "Definitely don't want to be party to that, but at the same time, I don't want to get you in trouble."

"You won't. They want us there. They're excited Marietta Travel is participating. I'll send some of my business cards with you, and an old driver's license for checking in."

"Do I need to dye my hair brown? Mandy could—"

"No, don't! It'd never be the same. And no one will say anything about the hair color, not when everyone is turning their hair blue these days. Just go and have fun and forget about Greg and what a two-timing schmuck he is, okay?"

"Easier said than done, but yes, that's the plan."

THE LAST TIME Quinn Douglas had flown into Jackson Hole he'd been with his former girlfriend, Alice, and her father Leo Sterling on their private plane, flying in from Seattle for Christmas at the Sterling's vast Wyoming ranch with the equally impressive, sprawling ten-thousand-square-foot "lodge."

By the time they'd arrived on December twenty-third,

the Sterling ranch house had already been prepped by staff for the holidays, with a fourteen-foot tree in the great room, and fresh green boughs wrapping the rough-hewn bannister railings. Gingerbread cookies had been baked and fires had crackled in all seven fireplaces. There had been a lot of eating and drinking and extravagant gift giving. Quinn had found Christmas with the Sterlings perfectly enjoyable—after all, it was his second holiday spent with them—but a Sterling Christmas was a far cry to his humble beginnings in Paradise Valley, Montana.

Last year, on Christmas Day, he drove to Marietta for an evening meal with his family—sister McKenna and her clan, brother Rory and his new bride. McKenna hosted a Douglas family dinner at her and Trey's house, and it was the complete opposite of the Sterling Christmas—noisy and chaotic with babies crying and kids fighting and lots of good-natured ribbing and laughter. There was no staff to do the work, thus everyone pitched in, with cooking and kids and cleanup.

Quinn enjoyed playing bachelor uncle, even on his back in front of the living room fire with his nieces and nephews crawling all over him. He'd loved being with his family, and he adored the nieces and nephews, but it made him question the future. His future.

His phone rang as he waited for his rental car to be brought around. He glanced at the number. *Alice.*

Quinn tensed and then took a deep breath and answered the call. Even though they'd broken up over the summer, she still stayed in close touch, in hopes that they might get back together. "Hey," he said, answering, the call.

"So you made it?" she asked.

"Just got here. Picking up my car now."

"I wish I was there. I love Jackson Hole."

"It is gorgeous," he agreed, suppressing the ambivalence he felt every time they talked.

Alice had wanted to marry him. She still wanted to marry him. They'd dated for almost three years, and she'd taken the breakup hard, feeling as if she'd invested a huge chunk of her life into him and she was still trying to get him back. There would be no going back. He didn't know how to explain it to her without hurting her more, and so he smashed his unease and tried to be supportive, hoping that eventually she'd meet someone new and be able to move on.

"Lots of snow?" she asked.

"It's been snowing all day."

"The powder would be amazing." Alice sighed wistfully. "We haven't had great snow in the Cascades yet, which reminds me why I've called. Dad is still interested in that resort. He knows they're struggling financially and he's considering making them an offer."

"I don't think they're looking to sell."

"But they would, for the right price."

"Your dad lowballs everyone."

"Come on, sweetie, that's not fair. He's just a tough negotiator, and it's what makes him so successful."

"Mmm." Quinn wasn't about to contradict her, because Alice had always been a daddy's girl, but Leo Sterling was ruthless, and he'd made a fortune by taking advantage of those who were desperate. It wasn't the way Quinn had been raised and it made him leery of the future. If he married Alice, he could walk out of professional sports and be set for life, not because of what he'd achieved, but because her father, Leo Sterling, had built a dazzling real estate empire of luxury properties across the world and was one of the wealthiest men on the West Coast. Quinn could leave baseball behind—and Alice was desperate for him to leave ball and get off the road—and then Quinn could become her father's right hand, the son he never had. It was all that Alice wanted.

And nothing Quinn wanted.

He tried to share with Alice his reservations, but she couldn't understand why he wouldn't want to be part of her family's company. His resistance to working with her family became an issue between them, and it made him question his commitment to her.

If he truly loved Alice, the shifting of his career shouldn't be so hard. If he loved Alice, he should be happy to stay in Seattle and become vice president of Sterling Luxury Resorts. It would be a cushy job. All the hard work would have been done for him. All he needed to do was show up, dress the part, wine and dine clients, shake hands, sign a few autographs and be the good son-in-law, Seattle Mariner third baseman, Quinn Douglas, baseball hero.

There was nothing about the job description that appealed, though.

"The car is here," he said, noting the black four-wheel-drive truck pulling up.

"So what shall I tell Dad? That you'll report back?"

"Alice, I'm here for me. I'm looking for investment opportunities for me."

"You're getting into property, too?"

"I'm looking for investments that make sense to me. This one is close to home—"

"It's five hours from your family, across the Tetons. I wouldn't call it convenient."

"I have a house four hours from here, and I like driving."

"Dad says they are in deep. They're not going to survive this year. You don't want to take on something like that. You could lose your shirt."

"I'm not looking to buy them. I'm looking to invest in them. Huge difference."

"Dad wants them. Don't undermine him."

"Peter Pace, the owner of Little Teton, is an old friend. I'm not going to stand by and let him go bankrupt if I can help."

"You played minor league ball with him. You barely knew him."

"We were roommates in single A ball. I knew him quite well."

NOT CHRISTMAS WITHOUT YOU

"But that was years ago. Don't throw your money away. Dad says—"

"Your dad is smart. He is. But his way isn't always the right way, Alice. We both know that. Goodbye."

Quinn hung up before she could reply and ground his teeth together. This was the part he couldn't stomach. Alice might be beautiful and smart and well connected, but she didn't understand that he came from a very different family, with different values. And maybe his parents had died when he was a teenager, but he was old enough to have internalized those values. People mattered. Kindness mattered. Integrity mattered.

Alice had a good side, and he admired her immensely for being ambitious and hardworking, but he wasn't ever going to be able to peel her away from Seattle, and he had family in Montana and it was his dream to one day return to Montana full time. When he broached the subject to Alice in early July, she recoiled, rejecting the idea of ever living in Montana permanently, and he suddenly had clarity on their relationship.

He could love someone, but it didn't make the relationship right.

He could want the best for someone, but it didn't mean that person was his person.

And so instead of proposing, during the July All-Star Break, he broke up with her. It had been five months since he ended the relationship but she was still hanging on, determined to get him back.

He had no plans to get back together with her. Ever. She was a great woman. She just wasn't his woman.

CHARITY HAD BEEN worried that forecast of snow would make the drive over the Teton Pass treacherous, but her seven-year-old Subaru handled the roads beautifully, and yes, the snow fell steadily, but there was no wind and her windshield wipers did a great job of scraping the window clean, keeping her view clear.

She'd armed herself with a thermos of coffee and mentally prepared herself for a long drive, but even with a stop for gas, she'd made it in less than four and a half hours, delighted to arrive at the privately owned Little Teton Resort before dark.

Parking her car out front in the area marked for reception, Charity headed into the lodge to check-in. The split-log lodge, built in the late 1960s, was more practical than luxurious, but the soaring ceiling featured sturdy beams, a fragrant Christmas tree in the corner, dark green garland swags over the various doorways, and an enormous wreath with a jaunty red bow over the stacked stone fireplace. The building's design was more utilitarian than some of the fancier lodges over the mountain in Jackson Hole, but the decorations were cheerful and inviting.

Check-in at the front desk was easy. She gave them Trisha's name and ID Trish had given her, and the friendly reception clerk handed over a key, a map of the property, and a welcome packet for the Little Teton fam.

"There's a welcome reception tonight for all the travel agents. The reception will be in this building upstairs in the Fireside Room." The clerk opened the map and drew some *X*s here and there, showing Charity where the Fireside Room was, and then where to park, and how to find her room as Charity wouldn't be in the main lodge, but in Aspen Lodge, one of the adjacent buildings.

The clerk leaned forward and whispered, "You're in my favorite building. It has the best coffee and chocolate in all of Little Teton Village. They have morning bakery items too, but they sell out quickly, so if you like a great chocolate croissant, go early." She glanced around and then dropped her voice even lower. "And maybe best of all, Seattle sports-writer Douglas Quincy is in the Aspen Building, too, on the ground floor, and he's gorgeous. As well as single. I know, because I asked."

"Thank you, but no," Charity answered with a rueful shake of her head. "I'm not looking for love. I've sworn off men until the new year."

"Why?"

"Penance for making bad decisions." Charity scooped up the paperwork and room key. "But thanks for the tip on the chocolate. Fortunately, I have not given sweets up."

Charity headed back outside to move her car. It was dark

now and lights were coming on, reflecting brightly off the freshly fallen snow. She drew a deep breath, inhaling the crisp cold air, excited to be at the Little Teton for the next five days. It had been a long time since she'd done something just for fun.

Using her map, Charity found her way to the lot behind the two-story Aspen Lodge and parked in one of the many open spaces. As she turned her engine off, she frowned as she surveyed the virtually empty parking lot. It was too quiet. Indeed, when she'd turned down the small Main Street she thought the entire ski town looked quiet. Low numbers had been a problem for the resort and that was why the Pace family had poured money into Little Teton, trying to refresh the resort and ski runs, but the word didn't seem to have gotten out yet.

Charity swung her backpack filled with books onto her shoulders and then lugged her big suitcase out of the trunk of her old Subaru, glad no one could see her mammoth suitcase. Winter clothes and snow boots took up a lot of room and then she also wanted to bring some cute clothes for the indoor activities. Just because she was single, didn't mean she couldn't still feel pretty.

One of the wheels on the suitcase no longer rolled, so she half carried, half dragged the case through the snow toward the lodge entrance. Yellow lamps made everything glow and she drew a deep breath, surprisingly excited to be here.

She'd never been to Jackson Hole, or any of the resorts

on this side of the Grand Tetons. It wouldn't be hard to appear enthusiastic for the fam trip because she really did want to learn about the resort and runs. Charity was determined to take great notes back so Tricia could sell Little Teton to her customers and everyone would be happy.

The backpack straps slid down her shoulders to her arms as she wrested the suitcase over a patch of ice.

"Let me help you," a deep male voice said from behind her, reaching an arm past her to lift the large case. "You've got your hands full."

"Thank you," she answered breathlessly, pushing the straps of the backpack up and then a tendril of hair out of her eyes to get a better look at him because first impression was, well, impressive. Second impression was just as positive. He was tall and fit and ruggedly good-looking with shaggy, dark blond hair, scruff on his square jaw, and high hard cheekbones.

"That's a big suitcase," he said, opening the front door and holding it for her, before following with the bag.

"A girl has to have options," she answered with a smile, glancing around the interior. The lobby of Aspen was small, but cozy, with two sets of hunter-green leather chairs, a fire crackling in the stacked stone hearth, and a collection of pine trees in the corner covered in tiny white lights. Huge glass jars filled with candy canes and peppermints decorated the mantel while a white wooden reindeer with a green wreath around its neck filled the low coffee table.

She nodded approvingly, backpack sliding off her shoulder once more. "I wasn't sure what to expect but this is cute."

"You'll like the rooms. They've obviously spent a lot of money trying to make it appealing and I think they've succeeded."

She gave up trying to keep the backpack on her shoulder and just let it slide to her feet. "Are you here for the travel agent trip?"

"I am, but I'm not a travel agent. I'm a writer."

So this was the sportswriter. The desk clerk had called him gorgeous, and he was. "Tricia Thorpe," she said shyly, extending her hand.

"Douglas Quincy," he replied, his big hand engulfing hers, fingers closing around hers.

His palm was so warm, and the touch of his skin sent a little jolt of electricity shooting up her arm. Charity quickly retracted her hand, and rubbed it on the back of her coat, trying to erase the tingling sensation. She'd have to be careful around Douglas. He was exactly what she didn't need, not at this point in her chaotic, confusing life. "Where's home for you?" she asked.

"Seattle, Washington."

"Oh, then you're the one to ask about coffee. I've heard there is a great coffee place in this building. Have you seen it?"

"You'll find the little café down that hall," he said, pointing to the left. "Elevators and rooms are to the right, and the heated pool is out the door down that little hall."

She flashed what she hoped was a confident smile. "Great. Well, I'd better get settled."

"You'll be at the welcome reception?"

Her pulse sped up, double time. "See you there."

QUINN WATCHED TRICIA disappear down the hallway with her massive suitcase and knapsack, her long blonde ponytail swinging.

She was pretty, really pretty, with a wide, uncertain smile and blue eyes that held more than a hint of wariness in them. Her suitcase looked as if he it hadn't been used in a long time, and her knapsack belonged to a day hiker rather than a world traveler. Quinn suspected she didn't get out and travel as much as her customers. If that was true, he was glad she was here. He didn't know why, but she struck him as someone in need of a break, and maybe some fun.

Quinn hadn't come for fun. When Peter Pace had reached out to Quinn about potentially investing in Little Teton, Quinn's immediate thought had been no. He didn't ski due to a clause in his contract, but it hadn't been a huge loss as he'd liked to ski as a boy, but it had never been a passion. Baseball had always been his thing, and he'd been lucky to turn it into a lucrative career.

But after thinking about Peter's request a bit more,

Quinn at least owed Peter the opportunity to show him what he'd done in Wyoming, which was why Quinn was here now, under the name Douglas Quincy. He wanted to see if there was a way he could help, but he wouldn't know the answer to that until he'd been here for the week.

THAT EVENING, CHARITY spotted Douglas the moment she entered the meeting room off the main lodge's lobby. He was the tallest person in the room, and incredibly easy on the eyes. He was also circled by a large group of women who seemed to find him utterly charming.

Charity smiled to herself and went to the beverage table to grab a bottle of water but then spotted the red and white wine and decided, a glass of red would be really lovely about now. She wasn't exactly nervous being here, but she was out of her element.

As she sipped her wine, she glanced around the room. From the way it'd been set up, she gathered that there would be a presentation. Two rows of chairs faced a podium and screen at one end of the room, while tables of food and drink were at this end.

She snagged some of the skewered meat sticks and cheese cubes before heading toward the chairs. If Tricia was here, she'd mingle with the other agents, but Charity didn't have Tricia's confidence. But then, Tricia did these familiarizations all the time as hotels and airlines used the free trips as a way to show off new airplane routes or properties, and Marietta Travel might be small, but Paradise Valley was filled with wealthy people who could afford to go where they wanted, whenever they wanted.

A shadow stretched over her. She glanced up to discover the sportswriter at her side, smiling. His smile was a thing of perfection—straight white teeth, great jaw, lovely mouth.

"Are you saving this row of seats?" he asked, gesturing to her row. "Or can you spare one for me?"

She tore her gaze from his mouth up to his eyes. Those were beautiful, too. He had not been shortchanged in the looks department. "I think I can spare a chair."

He sat down next to her and extended long, muscular legs. His legs were so long, his all-weather boots were hidden beneath the seat in front of him. "The ladies I just met are all from the West Coast, three from California, one from Oregon and another from Vancouver. They're very excited to be here."

"It's certainly a cute place," she answered.

"They hit the Ice Shack for dinner and recommended the fondue there. Actually, they raved about the cheese and a chocolate fondue."

She was amused by this conversation. Did big, muscular men like fondue? "I don't think I've ever had fondue."

"Never?"

She shook her head and sipped her wine. "Are you a fondue fan?" she asked innocently.

"I wouldn't say I'm a fan, but it's a fun thing to do on a ski trip. Do you ski?"

"I can get down the mountain but it's not particularly pretty. More survival skiing than anything."

She was rewarded with a laugh, and the deep, husky appreciative sound burrowed inside of Charity, warming her. He really was incredibly attractive, and it wasn't just his looks—which were exceptional—but it was his smile and laugh and the way he just seemed so much larger than life. More real, more alive somehow.

"Since you're not a travel agent, why are you here?" she asked, crossing her legs and opening her notebook. "Are you doing an article on ski resorts, or are you writing specifically about this one? What's the scoop?"

"I know the owner here. The resort needs publicity, and I thought I'd see if there was some way I could help them out."

"That's nice of you."

His broad shoulders shrugged. "I try to be nice."

She had a weakness for a man with a sense of humor, and he definitely had one. "I confess I don't really know a lot about Wyoming resorts." She lowered her voice so no one else would hear. "In fact, this is my first time here. I didn't even know that Little Teton existed."

"Jackson Hole gets most of the attention. Then for those who want to ski this side of the mountain, they usually hit Grand Targhee. Even though Little Teton Resort and the

Grand Targhee were built just five years apart back in the sixties, the Grand Targhee was just managed better, and found their customers, and kept them. Little Teton passed from one owner to another, and each owner did less and less to take care of the place. Peter Pace, the new owner, has poured money into this resort but they don't have a lot of bookings and they can't afford to go through the winter without revenue."

"Which is why we're all here."

He nodded. "I'm a little worried, though, as Peter can't compete with Jackson Hole, at least, not with those who want trendy and luxury. This place isn't going to be for the jet-setters who want to be seen."

"Not everyone wants to be seen. I know I've only just arrived, but I'd think it'd appeal to those who want great snow and the authentic Rocky Mountain ski experience."

"It'll be interesting to see how family friendly they are," he added.

She nodded as a pair of women squeezed past them to sit down in their row. Others were taking chairs in the row ahead of them.

"Have you gone on a lot of fam trips?" he asked.

"No, this is my first."

"So why this one?"

She glanced up into his handsome face with the piercing blue eyes and didn't know why she felt compelled to be honest. Maybe it was because the past few weeks had been so hard, or maybe it was the relief of being someone new, somewhere new. "I needed a break, and this seemed to be the perfect change of scenery. Work and vacation all in one."

"Is travel that hectic this time of year?"

"No, just my life right now." She made a face. "I have inadvertently become the queen of bad decisions."

"No."

"Yes."

He waited a moment, eyes narrowed as his gaze swept her face before lingering on her rueful smile. "What's the most recent bad decision?" he asked.

Charity hated the sudden ache in her chest. It was so stupid to let Greg hurt her and she forced a shrug, not wanting to let Douglas know just how bruised she felt. "Turns out my boyfriend wasn't as committed to me as he let me believe."

"What a schmuck. You're better off without him."

"I agree. Unfortunately, we work together so it's extra uncomfortable." She shook her head. "I should have known better. There's a reason why they tell you not to date anyone from work."

"Hopefully, he's just another agent and not your boss."

It took Charity a moment to process what he meant and then she grimaced. "Not my boss, thank goodness. I've made some mistakes in my time, but thankfully have never made that one."

Conversation was curtailed by the appearance of a man

at the podium. For the next ten minutes they watched a video about the history of skiing in Wyoming and the creation of the Little Teton Resort in the Grand Teton Mountains. The short film used old photographs and some home movie clips to convey the history of the resort, before seguing into the new owners' vision for Little Teton, and the developments they'd done since acquiring the resort two years ago. By the time the film was over, Charity wished she was a real travel agent who could send the resort dozens of guests.

"That was really interesting," she said to Douglas as the lights went back on and they were all excused to go enjoy the rest of their evening. "I loved the film, too. I'm glad they've added it to their website. I'll have everyone in the office watch it when I return."

They stepped out of their row so everyone else could escape. Resort staff were stacking the platters and collecting dirty dishes from a tray in the corner.

"What are your plans for the rest of the evening?" Douglas asked, as she added her empty wineglass to one of the big trays.

"Go back to my room and read."

"Read?"

She slipped her notebook into her purse. "I love to read."

"What kind of books?"

"Romance," she said a little defiantly, waiting for him to make fun of her.

He didn't, although the corner of his mouth lifted and his blue eyes gleamed. "Really?"

"Yes, really. I love that they always end happy. I love that in a romance the woman is just as important as the hero. In fact, I think she is the hero." Charity lifted her chin, expression challenging, again waiting for him to make a smart remark, but he just gave her another smile, creases fanning from his eyes.

"I'm not going to fight with you. We all have different ways to relax. I play Xbox. I even carry the console and controller in my suitcase when traveling. My girlfriend wasn't a fan, so I tried to play only when on the road, but sometimes it was the best way for me to unwind and unplug, necessary in my line of work."

"So we all have a guilty pleasure."

"Exactly. What was your boyfriend's? Do you remember?"

"Baseball."

"He played?"

"No. He's a die-hard Cubs fan. He had one of those sports packages and he'd watch almost every single game on TV, and baseball has a lot of games."

"Yes, I know."

"What was your girlfriend's guilty pleasure?"

"Shopping," he said without hesitation. "She was the very definition of a shopaholic. But she could afford it so I'm not judging."

"Wow. Lucky. That's one thing I don't do. I was raised in a family that didn't have very much, and it's still pretty tight."

"Travel agents don't earn a lot, do they?"

Charity thought of all the fun opportunities Tricia did have, working in her industry. "But there are lots of perks. Like this one. Being here." She glanced around and realized they were the only two left in the room that weren't staff. "I guess we should let them clean up without having to work around us."

"I know you've got your book waiting for you in your room," he said, as they stepped into the hall, "but I'm going to check out the Ice Shack and their incredible cheese fondue. Want to join me? We each have a dinner voucher and we can use it in any of the resort restaurants."

Douglas was handsome and smart and very appealing. She was enjoying his company a little more than she should. But this wasn't a dinner date; it was business. She was networking. "I think it's time to try my first fondue."

CHAPTER TWO

THE ICE SHACK looked empty when they arrived but a hostess appeared in a cute ski outfit and walked them to a table at the window overlooking the ice rink. The ice outside glowed blue and purple from colored lights, and the Ice Shack reflected the same colors, with white sculptural walls that looked like stacked blocks of ice, floor-to-ceiling columns made out of clear acrylic icicles, and the lighting was soft, with the same wash of lavender and blue lights like the outside ice rink.

"This is amazing," Charity said as they reached their white table with matching white chairs. "It is like the inside of an ice cave."

"Without the freezing temperature," he answered, holding her chair for her as she sat down. "I've been to a real ice bar and they're cold."

His fingers brushed her back as he assisted her chair forward. She couldn't remember the last time someone held her chair, or opened the car door. Not true. Her first love, Joe Wyatt, had been the same way. He was a cowboy from east of Pray in Paradise Valley and he'd been very protective. He was a great person, and he would have been a great husband and father—if she could have handled living in the middle of nowhere. But Montana winters were harsh, and the Wyatt ranch was high in the Absarokas. Even in good weather it was a thirty-minute drive to Marietta. In winter, it could be impossible. He couldn't change the location of the Wyatt ranch—it'd been in the family for eighty years—and she couldn't tear herself from her family. He hadn't understood, but then, he wasn't the one leaving everything behind. His grandfather and mother lived on the ranch. Three of his four brothers worked the ranch when not competing on the rodeo circuit. His whole world was high up in Paradise Valley whereas hers was Marietta.

She exhaled in a rush, wishing she'd stop thinking of Joe. Somehow her breakup with Greg had thrown her into a tailspin, making her question every decision, good and bad.

Douglas sat down across from her and looked at her. His brow creased. "What's wrong?"

She struggled to smile. "Careful. You'll get me talking and you might just get an earful."

"I have nowhere to go, and nothing to do."

"You really shouldn't encourage me."

"Why not? Maybe I want to hear everything."

"Seriously? Because I've been told that men find women's emotions terrifying."

He laughed, creases fanning from the corner of his eyes. "Not exactly terrifying, but they can be a little overwhelming for the novice. Fortunately, I have a sister—she's two years younger than me—and she helped me understand that women need words more than men. Sometimes she just needed to talk, and she'd feel better." He studied her for a moment, still smiling, and yet his blue gaze was warm, his expression kind. "So talk to me. What's upsetting you?"

"Because I'm a terrible judge of character, I now need to figure out what I'm going to do about work. I'm not sure if I can keep working with Greg, but if I look for a new job, my sister, Amanda, is going to beg me to come work for her, and please don't tell anyone I said this, but I think that would be worse than where I am now."

"Your sister is worse than Greg the Schmuck?"

"No. She's amazing. She's the best sister, and my best friend, and it's her dream that I go work for her salon, but it's not for me. It really isn't."

"You can't just tell her that?"

"I don't want to hurt her feelings, and it would. Amanda might be the baby in the family, but she's fierce. When she wants something, nothing stops her." Charity drew a quick breath. "I'm... not like that. I'm not driven and ambitious. It's kind of a problem. I honestly think it's what has gotten me into my current situation."

"Are there any other travel agencies in your area you could work at?" he asked.

And just like that, Charity remembered where she was, and who she was supposed to be. Tricia Thorpe. And Tricia loved her work, and loved travel, and if word got back to Marietta Travel that Tricia was looking for another job… oh, that would be terrible.

"No," she said more firmly, sitting up and squaring her shoulders. "I don't want to work anywhere else, and you know what, I'm not going to be chased out of a job I enjoy. I'm good at what I do, and if Greg doesn't like it, he can go, not me."

Douglas lifted his water glass and saluted her. "That's the fighting spirit."

They ordered fondue—cheese for starter and a chocolate dessert version to finish—and over glasses of wine and chunks of crusty bread swirled in decadent melted cheese they talked about their past relationships, discovering neither of them had been married or engaged, although they both had come close.

Answering Douglas's question, Charity said, "He did propose, but I couldn't say yes. I loved him, I did, but I knew we wanted different things and it would be a problem moving forward."

"Have you ever regretted your decision?" he asked.

"I've regretted letting him go because I've never felt that way about anyone since, but I still think I made the right decision. I need people more than he does. I need to be in town."

She twirled her fondue fork in the bubbling cheese in the copper-hammered pot. "What about you? What's your longest relationship?"

"The one that just ended this summer. We were together almost three years."

"Why did it end?"

"She wanted to get married and I didn't."

"Not the marrying sort?"

He didn't answer immediately. "I always planned on getting married one day, but it has to be right. I'd rather be single than in an unhappy marriage."

Charity watched him repeatedly stab a cube of bread. He seemed far more interested in stabbing it than eating it. "Why wasn't she the one?"

He was silent so long Charity wasn't sure he was even going to answer, and then he shrugged. "It was what you said. We wanted different things. Her vision for the future was different than mine."

"So what do you want? Do you know?"

"I want to be happy."

"Doesn't everyone?" she asked, before popping the hot cheesy bite into her mouth.

"You'd think so, but happiness can look very different to people. For me, it's not about money or lifestyle. It's not about impressing others, or catering to what people think. It's about being true to yourself and giving your best to those closest to you."

The cheese was hot and it took her a moment to swallow and be able to talk. "It's how it should be, isn't it?" she agreed. "Family should be the people we love most. The people we protect. But it doesn't always work out that way."

"Why do you think that is?"

"I guess it's easy to take your family for granted. But it's such a mistake. Family is everything. My sisters are everything. They've gotten me through really hard times."

"Tell me about your sisters."

"I have two. My older sister Jenny lives in Colorado with her husband, and my younger sister Amanda, or Mandy, lives just a mile from me. Mandy's my best friend. Growing up, we were two peas in a pod. We did everything together. She just got married in June." A lump suddenly filled her throat. "It's changed things a little bit, but I'm happy for her. She married a great guy. He adores her, and respects her, and Mandy deserves it."

"But you miss her," Quinn said quietly.

Charity blinked back tears. "I do. We still see each other every week, and yet, it's not the same. Maybe it's me, keeping my distance, but when we're all together I feel like a third wheel."

"Then just do things with her."

"I do, but it's not as often. Mandy adores him and she invites me to do things with them all the time. Sometimes I do, and sometimes I think they just need couple time."

"And they do, as they're newlyweds."

"I'm not jealous of her happiness, but I'm... lonely." She wrinkled her nose. "I shouldn't have said that, should I? I sound like a brat."

"No, you sound like someone who has always had a team, but her team has changed, and she's trying to figure out how to play the game on her own."

"Wow. You are a sports writer."

He laughed quietly, and yet his expression was sympathetic, which only made him even sexier.

"I do miss my team," she said softly. "Now that I think about it, I only started dating Greg after Mandy got married. Such a mistake."

"Hindsight is always twenty-twenty."

"Yes, and I can see now that instead of dating him, I should have used my free time to focus on my design work. That's my secret passion. I love fashion. I love designing clothes. Mandy has always been my favorite model. I created her wedding dress, and most of her wardrobe." She paused, grimaced. "I haven't made her anything since the wedding. I was planning on making her something for a Christmas party but haven't done it yet."

"What would you make?"

"Something glamorous. Mandy looks like a 1940s pinup. Very blonde and really beautiful."

"She can't be more beautiful than you. You're a stunning woman, Tricia."

Tricia.

Charity flushed, cheeks hot. She didn't even hear the compliment, too bothered by her deception. She wanted to tell him who she really was, but couldn't, not with him being a friend of the owner. There was no way Charity could risk getting Tricia in trouble. "Thank you," she murmured, and then not knowing what else to say, she grasped at the first thing that came to mind. "Have you stayed in touch with your girlfriend?"

"We talk now and then, and text a couple times a week," he answered.

"So you've stayed on good terms."

"She's a great person."

"Do you want to get back together?"

"No."

"Does she?"

He didn't answer, which told her plenty.

"Does she work at your magazine or paper, or wherever you work?" Charity persisted.

"No." He winked at her. "I know better than to date my coworkers."

His wink made her pulse quicken and her cheeks warm. She wished she didn't find him so attractive. Being friends with him would be easier without the sizzle of desire she felt every time she glanced into his face. "How did you meet her?"

"Alice?" His brow furrowed, and he paused, remembering. "We met at a fund-raiser, and we just clicked, and that was that."

"I bet she's beautiful."

"She is. Smart, too. Very focused, very ambitious. I admire her a great deal."

Charity bit into her lower lip, hiding her dismay because she wasn't ambitious. It was a problem, really. "So you don't regret the relationship?"

"Not at all. I learned a lot from our time together. I learned what I needed in a relationship and what I don't need. Alice is a wonderful woman, and I'm glad we had those three years together, but now it's time for the right relationship, the one that will hopefully lead to marriage and kids."

"You want a family."

"Most definitely."

She could see him with kids, and it gave her a little pang. "Did Alice not want children?"

"No, she did, but we had different ideas about how to raise them, and where to raise them. It worried me. Let's be honest, if we disagreed that much before we had our first child, I couldn't imagine the tension after."

"It's hard to grow up in a house filled with tension."

"I think you're smart to make sure it's right. That's why I'm determined to take my time from now on. No more jumping into relationships. No more dating just to date. It's not worth it."

He lifted his wineglass. "To waiting for the right one."

She clinked her glass against his. "I'll drink to that!"

THEY SPENT THE next day together as they explored the resort, their small group walking the hotel grounds, and then given a little tour of town. They had lunch at the pizza place, and then they were treated to a movie in the small, three-screen movie theater. It was a holiday film, a new version of *The Grinch*, and Charity could barely focus on the story, so aware of Douglas next to her.

She liked being next to him. She liked the feeling she got when he smiled at her, because she couldn't help smiling back. And when she smiled, she went warm and fizzy. She felt happy… happier than she'd been in a very long time.

As they left the movie and walked back to the lodge, Douglas mentioned how Little Teton was perfect for families. "If they renovated the old bowling alley, you'd have quite a lot for families to do here between skiing, sledding, ice skating, movies, and bowling. Everything is priced well, too."

"Do you think that's part of the problem, though?" she asked him. "That the Paces have tried to keep Little Teton affordable, and it's hurting their ability to recoup their investment?"

Douglas lifted a brow. "That's very insightful."

"You can't work in real estate—" She broke off, flustered, realizing she'd nearly given herself away. "I have a friend whose husband is always looking for investments," she added quickly. "They talk about this kind of thing a lot."

"Your friend and her husband are right. If the Paces

charged more for lodging and lift tickets, they'd certainly earn more. But would it drive away the customers they want?"

Charity and Douglas continued the conversation all the way back to the Aspen Lodge, and it amazed Charity at how much Douglas listened to her, and respected her opinion. Greg certainly never had. He'd always acted so superior.

"What did you study in school?" she asked Douglas, as he opened the front door of the lodge for her.

"Economics," he answered. "And you?"

"Communications."

"Maybe Peter should talk to you about how they could improve their marketing and public relations."

"Oh, I don't know that I'd have good ideas for him. It's been a long time since I was in school." She glanced at her watch, checking the time. They had several hours before dinner. "What are you going to do now?"

"I might get a workout in. And you?"

"Read." She grinned. "And then maybe check out the pool area and the hot tub."

"I might do the same in an hour."

"See you there."

He did join her at the outdoor pool, too. She was sitting submerged to her shoulders on the wide pool steps, steam rising all around her, as he arrived. His cheeks were still dusky from exertion and his eyes were bright.

She tried not to stare as he stripped down to board

shorts, but it was impossible not to notice his body. He had such an amazing body—a big, muscular chest and honed, chiseled abs, great legs, lovely muscular arms. He eased into the pool next to her, sinking into the warm water with an appreciative sigh.

"Have you tried the hot tub?" he asked, after dipping all the way under and surfacing again.

"I did but it wasn't much warmer than the pool," she answered, admiring the way his biceps bunched as he sluiced water back from his face.

"I could try to turn up the heat."

"That's against the rules. There is a whole list of rules posted by the hot tub."

"But if it's too cold?"

"I think it's a cost-saving measure."

"A hot tub is supposed to be hot."

"You could get in trouble."

"Who is going to see?"

"I wouldn't do it. It's not worth it."

"What are they going to do? Kick me out of the pool? Send me home? I'm not worried."

He climbed from the pool and walked behind the small screen blocking the pool equipment. The freezing air didn't seem to bother him at all. After a minute he returned, disappointed. "They've got the thermostat locked down. I can't get it higher."

The lodge door opened as he stepped back into the pool.

A middle-aged man wearing dark trousers and a matching vest came out, a resort name tag pinned to his vest. "It's against the rules to tamper with the pool controls," the lodge employee said irritably. "Please observe the posted rules, or refrain from using the premises."

Douglas smiled unapologetically, which didn't seem to go over well with the resort employee.

"What are your room numbers?" the man asked.

"Why? Are you going to report us?" Douglas drawled, sinking deeper into the water, and tipping his head back against the tiled edge of the pool.

"It's within my jurisdiction to fine you, or remove you from the premises."

Charity shot Douglas an alarmed glance but he seemed to find the whole thing amusing. "It's alright, buddy. No need to get worked up. I was just concerned that your hot tub isn't hot, but on the lukewarm side."

"It's not lukewarm. It's a very pleasant ninety-eight degrees."

"Don't most people prefer a hot tub closer to 104?"

"That's excessively hot, and dangerous when combined with drinking."

"But we're not drinking. And a little warmer would be nicer. Could we possibly request you set it to 102?"

"It's at a proper temperature right where it is. If you're not happy—"

"I'm happy, Phil. That is your name, right?" Douglas

interrupted pleasantly, his bright eyes gleaming with mischief. "I was just thinking I could be happier, but if that's not in your jurisdiction, I'm fine."

Charity could tell Douglas was enjoying himself. Poor Phil wasn't having such a good time. "We're good," she said, giving Phil a sunny smile. "And I'll be sure Douglas doesn't touch the controls anymore. Sorry about that."

Phil walked off in a huff and Douglas continued smiling as the door closed behind the resort employee.

"You almost got us thrown out of here," she said to him.

He shrugged, utterly unrepentant. "Phil could work on his customer service skills."

"I don't think he really cared about making us happy."

"Which is a problem for a place already struggling financially."

She swam toward him and propped herself on the wall. "Do you think the situation here is really bad?"

He was silent a moment. "I think this could be their last winter if something doesn't change."

"Can your friend sell?"

"It's an option, but he wouldn't get all his money back, and he's sunk everything into the place."

She squared her shoulders and gave a little nod. "Then we just have to make sure we help him find his customers. They are out there. We just need to help spread the word."

Douglas's gaze swept her face and he gave her a slow smile. "Challenge accepted."

There was something in his warm blue gaze that made her heart melt and then, when he smiled that slow easy smile, her pulse jumped and she felt an electric little zing throughout her body.

He was something, he really was. And she had to be careful, so careful, because falling for him would be serious trouble.

HE REMAINED SERIOUS trouble, too, as during the next three days they continued sitting next to each other during presentations, and walking side by side during activities. They always ended up at the same table for meals, and he became her plus one in the chairlift up the mountain, and then again for the sleigh ride that circled the frozen lake.

It had been a long time since anyone made her feel so good about herself and Charity told herself to be grateful, and to focus on the moment because outside this lovely little bubble of Wyoming, they had nothing in common. There was no point in even considering more with Douglas. He was a city sportswriter, and she was a small-town girl, and if she wasn't willing to move thirty minutes away to the Wyatt ranch in Paradise Valley, how could Seattle be an option? It wasn't. And he wasn't. And yet the attraction was always there. She never felt more alive than when he was close.

Just watching him enter the room made her heart beat a little faster, and when he looked at her, she couldn't help but smile.

He was beautiful, and smart, funny and kind. Kinder to her than any man had been in years. Maybe that was the part that bowled her over. He was truly the complete package, possessing strength and warmth and surprising humility.

And now their trip was nearly over. This was their last night in Wyoming. Tomorrow they'd say goodbye.

Charity stepped off the ice rink to relace her boot, wishing she'd brought her own skates from home as she was finding it hard to get this pair to fit properly. She loved ice skating, too. It was actually something she could do well, and she was eager to show off a little for Douglas, who was out on the ice already, assisting some of the older women. Tonight's party at the ice rink was the final activity and she smiled as he shifted from one timid travel agent to the other, steadying wobbly skaters, and encouraging others to let go of the railing.

And then Douglas lifted his head and looked at her, and gave her that smile of his that made her pulse jump and her body hum. Thank goodness she came this week.

She rose from the wooden bench and stepped out onto the ice, and it felt like she had wings on her feet as she skated toward him. He held out a hand to her and a rush of pleasure swept through her as Douglas took her hand, and they skated around the ice.

He lifted an eyebrow at her, as they circled a second time. She arched a brow back, daring him, and in wordless agreement. They picked up speed, skating faster, feet crossing, blades scraping as they pushed through the turns, the cold night air filling their lungs. This, she thought, cheeks burning, heart pumping, was pure joy.

They were making their fourth sweep when one of the agents limping around the side tried to pass another agent, and somehow went staggering toward the middle of the ice instead of back to the railing. The agent yelped as she sailed out of control, arms flapping. Her terror created panic in the others and before Charity fully understood what was happening or why, there were travel agents falling right and left, littering the ice.

Douglas tried to slow the very first agent, but she flung herself at him, bringing them both down.

Charity started to laugh, and kept laughing as she glanced around the ice. Everyone was down. Not a single person—but her—remained on their feet.

And then Douglas reached up, caught her sleeve and pulled her down, too. She didn't fall hard, but the ice was cold and she felt the chilly dampness through her knit leggings. "That's so unfair," she protested as she scrambled back to her feet. "I'll get you back, Douglas. Just you wait."

He gave her a look that made her go all warm and mushy on the inside and then he was drawing the older ladies up off the ice, one by one.

Finally the ice was clear and Charity leaned on the wall, watching Douglas skate back to her. His gaze locked with hers, his blue eyes so warm.

She felt a thrill as he neared her. He wasn't hers, but he was. She'd always remember this week. Douglas had been such great company.

He skated off the ice and took a position at the wall next to her, his big frame brushing hers as he leaned against the railing. He didn't move away, either. He stood there, touching her and it felt right. Her heart raced. She wanted his arms around her. She wondered how he kissed.

Charity tried not to stare at his mouth. Not easy when he was standing this close, and his lips were just above hers, those firm lovely lips curved in a rueful smile.

"Planning your revenge?" he teased her, reaching out to pluck a long tendril of blonde hair from her cheek before smoothing it back behind her ear.

"Just you wait."

"So you keep saying."

"It'll be good."

"I hope so." And his smile grew wider, whiter.

Her chest seized, air bottling in her lungs. She had to be careful. She wasn't being careful. She was feeling too much, falling too hard, too fast. She wasn't strong enough to be hurt again.

Charity made a show of wiping the frost from her mittens and then brushed more ice from her backside. "That was epic out there," she said, trying for a lightness she didn't feel. "It was like roller derby ice-skating."

"Apparently Marianne used to skate, a very long time ago," he said, referring to the California travel agent that had careened across the outdoor rink, wildly out of control.

"Thankfully you broke her fall."

"I was terrified she'd break a hip."

"The dangers of putting seniors on the ice."

"And beautiful women like you," he added, tugging on her knit cap. "Are you okay? Break anything? Hip, elbow, knee?"

His touch sent a frisson of pleasure through her. "No." She smiled up at him. "Despite my encounter with the ice."

"I couldn't have you feeling left out."

"You mean you couldn't bear to have me still standing, when you were on your butt?"

"I was just looking out for you. I wanted you to know you will always be on my team."

His team.

Charity was so close to telling him the truth. She wanted to come clean and confess she wasn't Tricia Thorpe from Marietta Travel but Charity Wright, the receptionist at Melk Realty, but she'd made Tricia a promise and she'd keep her promise. "Thanks for putting me on your team," she said. "It's been fun."

"I'm not saying goodbye to you, kiddo. You're stuck with me, you know."

She smiled crookedly, touched, but aware it wouldn't play out that way. He might mean to stay in touch but things would come up. Feelings would change. This here at Little Teton was just what it was—a brief escape, an innocent romance—which was never meant to last in the real world.

"By the way," he added, "you can skate."

"I was thinking the same thing about you," she answered.

"I played a lot of hockey growing up," he said.

"Who knew?" she murmured, transfixed by his face, and his lips, wanting his mouth on hers, wanting to feel his kiss.

"When do you head back to Seattle?" she blurted, trying to focus on anything but his lovely face so very close to hers.

"Next week."

"What will you do until then?"

"Poke around here, do a little more research."

"I can't wait to read your article. You'll have to send me a link once it's—" She broke off as Marianne appeared and gave Douglas a grateful hug for saving her.

"My pleasure," he assured her gallantly.

Marianne beamed. "Your mother raised you right. You're such a gentleman. Tell her I approve."

His smile faded. His head momentarily dipped. "Will do," he said gruffly.

He was quiet after Marianne and her friends continued on. Charity looked up at him, wondering what had happened to change the mood. He'd been so relaxed a moment before but he suddenly seemed pensive.

"You okay?" she asked.

He nodded. "Yeah." He glanced out at the still-empty rink. "Do you want to get back out there, or have you had enough?"

She swiped her still-damp backside. "I think I'm done."

"Wish we had another couple days here," he said. "I've enjoyed this here with you."

"You were just the tonic I needed. Thank you."

"You're such a sweetheart."

She didn't know which made her more breathless, his deep voice or the words he'd said. *You're a sweetheart.* Somehow he made it sound like the most wonderful endearment she'd ever heard.

"You deserve to be happy," he added. "Demand happiness from life. Don't accept anything less."

The lump was back in her throat. He had this incredible ability to make her feel special and warm, gloriously warm. "I'll remember that."

He smiled down at her. "Do."

HE REALLY NEEDED to stop smiling at her. He was making her feel things and she couldn't possibly feel more, not when she was already tingling from head to toe. "Did you play other sports besides hockey?"

"Football, basketball… baseball."

"Did you play sports in college?"

"I did."

"When did you stop playing to be a writer?"

"When I realized you can't play forever."

She grimaced. "True. You have to pay bills."

He laughed, a big laugh that was another deep rumble, and then his head dropped and his mouth covered hers.

The kiss was light and yet electric. She felt every little bit of her come to life.

He deepened the kiss, her lips parting beneath the pressure of his, and her head spun.

This kiss made her yearn for happiness and magic. If only happy-ever-afters really did come true. Because at thirty she was beginning to be afraid, wracked with doubt that the happy-ever-after would happen for her.

And just like that, reality returned.

She remembered who she was and where she was and this beautiful, magical kiss was a mistake. "I'm sorry," she whispered, pulling back. "As much as I want to kiss you, I shouldn't. My life is a mess and this isn't going to help."

"No, I'm sorry." He took a step back, putting space between them.

"It's the timing," she said. "If the timing was different, or we lived closer, maybe it'd make more sense." She swallowed hard, feeling completely ridiculous because she'd wanted his kiss, and the kiss had been incredible. "I hope this doesn't mean we can't still be friends. I could use you as a friend—"

"I already told you, we're on the same team. You're stuck with me."

She struggled to smile. "Good."

"And I am sorry about the kiss. I totally misread the situation. I'm embarrassed—"

"Don't be. I wanted you to kiss me." Her lips twisted, her expression glum. "The problem was, you kiss really good. Far too good."

For a moment there was just silence, and for the first time since they met, it wasn't an easy, comfortable silence, and it crossed Charity's mind that it was already changing between them.

All it had taken was a kiss.

She shouldn't have wanted his kiss. She shouldn't have savored his attention. She'd come to Little Teton to escape the fire, not throw herself headfirst into the frying pan.

"It would be great to stay in touch. That way if I'm ever in Seattle, we could have dinner, or if you're ever this way again, we could meet for a drink or coffee."

"That would be great," he said. "Where do you live?"

"Montana. A little town outside Bozeman."

He gave her an odd look. "What's the name of your travel agency?"

"Marietta Travel."

"You're from Marietta?"

"You've heard of it?"

His expression was almost incredulous. "I have."

CHAPTER THREE

H AD HE HEARD of Marietta? Of course he had. It was
his hometown.

Back in his room, Quinn stretched out on his bed, aware
that everything had just become more complicated. If Tricia
looked him up, she'd discover there was no Douglas Quincy,
at least no sportswriter in greater Seattle named Douglas
Quincy.

Quinn didn't like deceiving people, much less people
from his hometown. Marietta had been good to him, and
people had rallied around his family after the tragedy on the
Douglas ranch. He had nothing but respect and appreciation
for Marietta, so the last thing he wanted to do was deceive
someone who knew the real him.

Thinking of Marietta, and his years at Marietta High
School, Quinn remembered a Colton Thorpe. Quinn had
played sports with Colton, a kid who had equal parts talent
and anger. The anger had won out, and Colton gave up
organized sports to get into trouble.

Quinn didn't know what had become of Colton, but he
couldn't help thinking that Tricia might be related to him. A

sister, or a cousin, possibly? Either way, he needed to explain things, and come clean with her about who he was, and why he was there in Wyoming, because he wouldn't be writing about the ski town.

He liked Little Teton a great deal, and spending the past five days with Tricia had made it even more special. Tricia was an amazing woman.

Was he disappointed she wanted to keep things platonic? Absolutely. He liked her, a lot, and all he wanted was to get closer to her, not keep his distance. He couldn't remember when he was this attracted to anyone. He wasn't even sure he'd felt this chemistry with Alice.

He left bed early the next morning and went to her room, wanting to catch her before she left. But she didn't answer the door and when he checked with the front desk, they said she'd already gone, leaving just after dawn.

Disappointment swept through him, and he kicked himself for not going to her room last night. Why had he waited?

Marianne, the travel agent from California, approached Quinn to say goodbye. "You look so lonely," she teased him. "Where did your cute little girlfriend go?"

"Home," he answered.

And then it struck him. Home. Tricia had gone home, to Marietta. Which meant, he knew just where to find her.

CHARITY COULDN'T HAVE asked for more perfect conditions

to drive home. The Teton Pass was clear, the wind was calm, and the rising sun made the dramatic mountain peaks glitter. Snow dusted the huge conifers making her think of white frosting. There was no ice on the road either. Her car handled the climb and descent beautifully.

She was lucky, she told herself as the miles accumulated. She was lucky to have such ideal weather for driving home. Lucky to have had a break from work. Lucky to have missed the Marietta Stroll where Greg was escorting his new girl-friend about.

And lucky to have met Douglas.

Her pulse jumped just thinking of him. Douglas Quincy had been absolutely lovely in every way. Meeting him at Little Teton had been rather like a perfect holiday romance, without the romance ending. But that was okay. She appre-ciated the story elements. Handsome stranger, playful activities, wonderful chemistry, and then the quick, bitter-sweet goodbye because they were off in different directions.

Maybe one day they'd see each other again. Maybe one day the timing would be better.

Or, maybe more realistically, this would just end up be-ing a very sweet, special memory for her to cherish.

Charity adjusted her sun visor, blocking out the bright morning glare, and used her car's Bluetooth to call her sister, not sure if Amanda would be at work yet, but Amanda answered her cell phone.

"Where are you?" Amanda asked.

"Back in Montana, still driving, a couple hours away," Charity answered.

"How was the ski resort?"

"Really good. Super cute little place. I'm glad I went. I've lots of notes for Tricia."

"You sound happy."

"I had fun."

"Tricia said everybody would probably be on the older side."

"Lots of older people, but there was a hot guy. We hung out together."

"And he's a travel agent?"

"No, he's a sportswriter, but he was there to get the resort some coverage."

"And he was good-looking?"

"Gorgeous. Tall, built, handsome as heck."

"Where does he live?"

"Seattle."

"But I'm sure he travels."

"I don't, though."

"Then why are you so happy?" Amanda asked.

"He was just... lovely."

"He was chivalrous, too. He opened doors and held my chair and helped me with my coat. He even tied my scarf once and it was just sweet because he looks so manly. Like big, rugged muscles everywhere, and then he was such a gentleman."

"You're smitten."

"I'm just grateful I met him because I realize that no one has treated me so well since Joe and I broke up, and that was an important epiphany. Next time I date someone, I want to be treated well. I want more of a man, not less."

"That's exactly right. You deserve more, not less."

"I realized something else," she added. "I'm letting fear hold me back. I'm afraid I'm not good enough so I've stopped making clothes for anyone but you. I've stopped designing altogether. I think that's a mistake."

"I've been telling you that for ages."

"But of course I don't believe you because you're my sister and a fan of everything I do."

"I'm a fan because you're good, not because you're related to me."

"Maybe I should advertise in the *Courier*, and try to pick up some custom orders here and there, just for the fun of it."

"And the income. The extra income would give you more independence. You should have your own place. A two-bedroom apartment or a little house down by the high school. You could take the second bedroom and turn it into a sewing room."

"But Mom and Dad need someone to look after them."

"Charity, they want your money. They don't necessarily want you."

Charity winced.

"I don't mean to be harsh, but we're terrible codependents," Amanda added quietly. "We don't help them by hovering over them, watching for every misstep, and it's not healthy for us."

"You didn't used to feel that way," Charity said lowly.

"Tyler has helped me with perspective. Getting married has made me look hard at the way we were raised, and just because we were raised a certain way, doesn't make it healthy, or right."

Charity didn't answer.

"Come over to the salon after work Wednesday night. Let's have a proper girls' night," Amanda said more gently. "It'll be like the old days when it was just you and me against the world."

"That would be wonderful. I'll bring the wine. Should I also pick up some appetizers?"

"I've got a good bottle of red here, and we'll just have a pizza delivered. It feels like forever since we really talked."

"I know."

QUINN SPENT ANOTHER two days in Wyoming, visiting different ski resorts in Jackson Hole to complete his research, before packing up the rental truck and heading north to Marietta.

When he first flew into Jackson Hole, he hadn't planned on hitting Marietta this trip, but now that he knew who Tricia was, he needed to see her and explain things. And not just to explain things. He needed to see her, period.

The fact was, he missed her. These past few days without her had been long, and boring. Little Teton lost its magic without her, and even a day trip to Jackson left him irritable. He didn't want to wander around the town on his own. He wanted Tricia with him. He wanted her hand in his, and he wanted to make a bad joke just to see her smile.

He had a sneaking suspicion he was falling for her. More than a sneaking suspicion. He wanted her, and he sensed she was interested in him, but her fears over failed relationships made her hesitant to get too close to him.

He understood that, and respected it, appreciating her caution, but if Quinn had learned anything about life it was that fate was fickle and time was short. If he wanted something—or someone—he went after it.

Which was why he was heading to Marietta now.

QUINN'S BIG LOG cabin home in Paradise Valley was on the way to Marietta, and he stopped at the sprawling house to shower and shave. While standing at the living room window with its expansive views of the Gallatin Mountain range and icy Yellowstone River snaking through the valley floor, he sent a text to his brother and sister letting them know he'd just arrived in Montana, and he'd be here for the night before flying out of Bozeman tomorrow.

"Want to come over for dinner?" his sister McKenna imme-

diately texted.

"I don't want to put you out," he replied. *"Let's just go some-where easy so you can sit and relax."*

"I can do that. How about Rocco's?" she texted back, before adding, *"I know you love their gnocchi. I'll check in with Rory, but let's plan on me making a reservation for six?"*

"Deal." He hesitated, before texting, *"Can you add one more to the reservation? I might have a plus one."*

"Is Alice with you?"

"No."

Quinn smiled, certain he could feel his sister's wheels turning, but he wasn't going to mention Tricia to her, at least not yet.

In good weather, it was an eighteen-minute drive from his house to town, but the icy roads had trucks going even slower.

He exited for Main Street and downtown Marietta looked just as it always did in December. Quaint. Charming. Festive. He was sure the Marietta Stroll had just taken place this past weekend. The red brick buildings lining Main Street were still decorated with little white lights and wreaths and boughs of greenery. Marietta had been lovingly pre-served, recently written up in a national magazine as one of America's hidden gems. Marietta was a gem, too, but he had a complicated relationship with the town. Folks in small towns knew too much about their neighbors, and people in Marietta most definitely knew too much about him, and his family.

In Seattle, he'd escaped his legacy as "one of those Douglases." On the field, no one cared about his past, and no one bothered bringing up the tragedy. The broadcasters had learned to leave it alone and the general public had forgotten that there had even been a "Paradise Valley Ranch Invasion." It was only here, in Marietta, that people remembered. It was here that people looked at him and remembered that he had been the only one who'd survived the shooting.

Quinn spotted Marietta Travel and parked his rental car out front. Opening the door to the travel agency, his gaze swept the interior. Marietta Travel had been on Main Street for as long as he could remember and in the early days of his career, Mrs. Ferguson, the former manager, would book all his travel. He glanced around the small office with the trio of desks in the front with another desk in a glassed-in office at the back. Mrs. Ferguson had retired years ago and he didn't recognize anyone at the desks, nor did he spot Tricia's long blonde hair and elegant profile.

Maybe Tricia was at lunch, or maybe she was in the bathroom or a storage room. He asked for her at one of the front desks. The older woman pointed to the glassed-in office at the rear.

"That's Tricia's office," the woman said. "Want me to get her for you?"

Quinn frowned as he gazed at the brunette sitting at the desk behind the glass wall. She wore her hair in a sleek ponytail and she looked to be the right age, but she wasn't

Tricia. She looked nothing like his Tricia. "Maybe I have the name wrong. I'm looking for Tricia Thorpe. She was just in Wyoming on a travel agent familiarization this past week."

The woman's forehead creased. "That is Tricia Thorpe. She's our manager. But she wasn't on a travel agent familiarization in Wyoming or anywhere else. She was here all week."

"It can't be. I was with Tricia at the Little Teton Resort, and Tricia is slim and blonde, with long hair, really pretty hair."

"Oh." The woman's eyes widened. "*Oh.* I think I understand." She rose from behind her desk, giving him a quick, sympathetic smile. "Why don't you come with me? I'm sure, uh, Tricia can clear this up."

He nodded grimly and followed her to the glass door.

"Can I help you?" the brunette asked, gesturing for him to take one of the two chairs opposite her desk.

"I'm looking for Tricia Thorpe," he said.

"I'm Tricia Thorpe," she answered with a quick smile. "And I think I know who you are. Quinn Douglas, yes?"

He swallowed around the uncomfortable lump in his throat. "Yes."

"Are you interested in booking some holiday travel—"

"Little Teton Resort," he interrupted, flatly. "They claim you were there this week and yet your agent up front said you've been here all week."

Tricia's smile faded. "I see."

"Do you? Because I don't."

Tricia exhaled slowly. "It's kind of convoluted." She stood up. "Want coffee or anything?"

"No." His arms folded across his chest. "So if you weren't in Wyoming, who was at the ski resort pretending to be you?"

Tricia sat back down. "Charity. Charity Wright."

The name was unfamiliar. "Is she from Marietta?"

"Yes. She's just younger than you. Do you remember Jenny Wright? She would have been your grade in school I think."

It took Quinn a second to picture a petite, slim blonde girl with big brown eyes. "I think so." His brow creased. "Blonde?"

Tricia nodded. "All three Wright girls are blonde and pretty. Jenny is the oldest. Amanda is the youngest. Charity is the middle sister."

Charity Wright. He silently repeated her name. The middle Wright. And suddenly he could remember Carol Bingley, Marietta's town gossip, making little digs about the Wright girls being all wrong. Was Charity one of those Wright girls who'd been mocked for being all wrong? "Mrs. Bingley didn't like the Wrights, did she?" he asked abruptly.

"No."

"Why didn't she?"

"The family struggled. Mr. Wright was a janitor at the high school and had... problems. He was eventually fired because of those problems."

Quinn flashed back to high school and the nice custodian who didn't mind if the boys were in the gym shooting baskets late because it meant he could hide away in his closet and drink.

They all knew he was drinking all the time.

Quinn's chest tightened, as air bottled in his lungs. He should have just gone back to Seattle where he was the Mariner's third baseman. "I remember," he said quietly.

"Charity is a really good person. In fact, she's one of the best people I know."

"You don't need to defend her. I'm not mad at her. I'm trying to find her to apologize."

Tricia suddenly looked worried. "What happened?"

"It's between her and me. But tell me, why was she there as you? She used your name the entire time."

"I was invited to attend the fam but I couldn't go, and they really wanted Marietta Travel represented so I sent Charity in my place."

"So she *is* a travel agent?"

Tricia shifted, uneasy. "She worked here for a summer years ago, but she's not affiliated with Marietta Travel right now."

"Why send her in your place?"

"Charity was having a hard time and I thought it'd be good for her to get out of Marietta for a few days and we could learn about the improvements made at the Little Teton Resort. It seemed like a win-win."

Everything Tricia was saying lined up with what Charity had told him at the resort, which only made him feel worse.

He rose from his chair and paced the length of the small office, before going to stand at the glass window with the view of the office and the agency's front door. "You know her well?"

"I grew up next door to the Wrights. Charity and I are still neighbors on Chance Avenue. And Jenny—the one you went to school with—married my brother Colton three years ago. So we're not just friends, but family."

"Is that where she is now? At her house on Chance Avenue?"

"No. She works—" She broke off, expression stricken.

"Where?"

Tricia shuffled the papers on her desk, cheeks reddening. "I think I've said too much as it is."

"I want to talk to her."

Tricia kept moving papers around before stacking them into a tidy pile. "Give me your number and I'll pass it on."

"I need to talk to her."

She avoided meeting his gaze. "I don't know what to tell you."

"No problem. I'll figure it out for myself." And then with a half nod in her direction he walked out.

TRICIA CALLED CHARITY'S cell phone the moment Quinn

walked out of the travel agency office. The phone rang so long Tricia was afraid that it would go to voice mail, but finally Charity answered.

"Sorry," Charity whispered. "Greg and Sam were having a conversation near my desk and I couldn't pick up right away. Everything okay?"

"I don't know." Tricia hesitated. "I just had an interesting visitor. I'll give you three guesses as to who might have stopped by to see me."

"I don't have time for guessing games. Why don't you tell me," Charity answered wearily.

"You okay?" Tricia asked. "You don't sound very happy."

"Greg is being exhausting. He's constantly watching me and hovering around my desk, giving me pointless tasks... things he could easily do himself, but now won't."

"He's a jerk."

"You warned me. I didn't listen." Charity sighed. "Never mind all that. Tell me who came to see you."

"Quinn Douglas."

"Seattle Mariner Quinn?"

"The very one."

"He wanted you to book him a trip?"

"Well, no. He said he spent last week with you at the Little Teton Resort—"

"No. It was all travel agents, thirteen women, one man, and then a sportswriter."

"Are you sure? Because he said he'd spent the week hanging out with you. He, um, seemed to think you were me."

Silence stretched. "What does he look like?"

"What do you mean, what does he look like? He's gorgeous. Tall, built, really built, all body—" She broke off, hearing Charity's faint choke. "And he's looking for you," she concluded.

"That makes no sense. I didn't spend last week with Quinn Douglas." She dropped her voice, aware that Greg was standing in his doorway watching her. Again. "My friend is a sportswriter named Douglas Quincy—oh. Oh, *no*." She made a rough sound. "Douglas Quincy. That's pretty much just Quinn Douglas backward."

"Yep."

Charity exhaled hard. "I can't believe it. Quinn. Douglas. Oh dear."

"That sounds serious."

"It's not. I'm just… shocked. Blown away, actually."

"Did you two hook up? I wouldn't blame you if you had. He is fine. Like, seriously, unbelievably fine—"

"I know what he looks like, and no, we didn't hook up. We were just friends."

"So why was he here in my office asking for you? Well, not you but me, because he thought you were me."

"I don't want to talk about him, Tricia. I went on the trip to escape heartache and, instead, I flung myself from the fire into the frying pan."

"I thought you said nothing happened."

"Nothing happened." Charity's voice rose and cracked and she made an effort to lower it. "But it didn't mean…" She drew a slow, unsteady breath. "It didn't mean that for a moment I didn't kind of… care. I didn't want to care, but you saw him. He is really handsome. And you talked to him. He is so likable. He is… was… wonderful. At least, he was wonderful until he kissed me—"

"So you did kiss?"

"Yes, just once, but it was enough for me to realize he's trouble. Serious trouble. And I can't do more trouble. I can't have my heart stomped on anymore."

"How does he kiss?"

"It doesn't matter. He's not for me. He's a professional baseball player.

"He lives in Seattle. He travels all the time. And, heck, if I can't even trust my boyfriend in Marietta to be faithful, how can I trust Quinn Douglas?"

"Quinn is a great guy."

"Because why? All the newspapers say so? Because his fans love him?"

"We grew up with him, Charity."

"Maybe you did, but I didn't. And I'm not interested in him."

"But you were at Little Teton."

"I might have been mildly interested in the sportswriter named Douglas, not the Quinn Douglas from Paradise

Valley."

"He's one and the same, girl."

Silence stretched and then Charity groaned. "Did you know who he was the moment he walked in to the agency? Or did he have to introduce himself?"

"I knew who he was." Tricia heard the soft, muffled curse at the other end of the line. "Why does it matter, Charity?"

"Because if I knew sports and followed sports, I would have recognized him, and none of this would have happened. I wouldn't have spent so much time with him, and I most definitely wouldn't have kissed him." Her voice deepened, growing husky. "I am pathetic. I am the most useless pathetic—" She broke off, before adding faintly, "Oh, no. Tricia, he's here. He's *here*. Why did you tell him where I worked?"

"I didn't. I swear."

"Then how did he find me?"

"I don't know."

CHAPTER FOUR

IT WASN'T OFTEN that Quinn Douglas felt played, but he felt a little played right now.

He'd come to Marietta thinking he was tracking down Tricia Thorpe to apologize for misleading her, and then planning to invite her to dinner with his family, and instead he was chasing a beautiful blonde receptionist named Charity Wright who had told him dozens of stories in Wyoming and now he didn't know if any of her stories were true.

Fortunately, it hadn't taken a lot of work to find Charity. One call to his sister McKenna and he learned where Charity worked, just two blocks north of the travel agency at Melk Realty on Main Street. Good old Main Street.

Quinn stepped inside the real estate office, and there she was at the reception desk, on the phone, looking blonde and beautiful, and guilty as heck.

"Hello, gorgeous," he said as she swiftly hung up and shoved her mobile phone into a desk drawer.

She rose from behind her desk, her cheeks dark pink. "Hello, *Douglas Quincy*," she said, emphasizing the name with an extra helping of sarcasm.

The corner of his mouth pulled. Was that the best she could do? He closed the distance, ignoring Sam Melk who'd come to his doorway, and another dark haired man in a suit and tie who was filling his doorway. "You're not Tricia Thorpe," he said, voice pitched low to keep the others from hearing.

"And you're not a sportswriter," she countered defiantly.

Her fierce tone made his lips curve and, as he stood next to her desk, gazing down at her, he had this odd thought— he should keep her.

And then another odd thought. He was here because she was supposed to be his.

Quinn Douglas had never chased a woman in is life. He hadn't needed to, and yet he thought he'd do just about anything to give Charity time to know him and trust him.

He'd felt protective of her at Little Teton, and he'd been drawn to her a little more every day until that last night when he kissed her, and knew that she was why he was there.

It wasn't the struggling resort that needed him. It was this beautiful woman who called herself the queen of bad decisions.

Kissing her, he'd felt hope, but also conviction. The kind of knowledge he'd felt growing up playing ball. He knew he was supposed to play. He knew what he was supposed to do. He felt that now.

If they weren't standing in the middle of Sam Melk's office Quinn would kiss her again. Being near her made everything seem possible. "No," he said with a wry smile, "not a sportswriter, but weirdly, we're both from the same small town. It's too coincidental, don't you think?"

"Yes," she said firmly. "I don't like it."

Quinn glanced from her to Sam Melk who was rapidly approaching. "Hello, Sam."

The realtor extended his hand. "Quinn, good to see you. What can I do for you?"

"Just stopped by to see Charity."

"I didn't know you'd stayed in touch with Charity."

Quinn shot a warm smile in her direction. "Thanks for giving her time off so we could catch up in Wyoming."

"Uh, that's—" Charity started to protest.

Quinn continued, ignoring her interruption. "We had a fantastic time. Great steaks at the Grizzly Den. Amazing fondue at the Ice Shack. A sleigh ride around the lake. I highly recommend Little Teton Resort." He glanced from Sam to the dark-haired guy hovering in the background. "I don't think I've met you," he said to the other man. "Quinn Douglas," he added, extending his hand.

"Greg Bartlett," the realtor answered, coming forward. "I'm newer to Marietta, but of course I've heard all about you. The Mariners aren't my team but you're a legend around here."

"Let me guess? Cubs fan?" Quinn asked, giving Greg's hand a firm squeeze and was pleased to see the other man wince slightly.

"Yes. How did you know?"

Quinn hated having to be civilized. "Lucky guess." He released Greg's hand and glanced over at Charity who was pressing her hands together and looking wildly uncomfortable.

"Did you tell them about the little chocolate place at the Aspen Lodge, Charity?" he added cheerfully. "Didn't you say it was as good as Copper Mountain chocolates?"

"I said it was almost as good. I didn't say it was as good." Charity's cheeks had turned pink. She cleared her throat. "Want to step outside? I'm sure Sam wouldn't mind. You probably want a coffee before you get on the road."

"Oh, I'm not heading anywhere tonight," Quinn answered. "I've only just arrived."

"We have coffee here," Sam interjected. "Charity wouldn't mind making a fresh pot. She makes great coffee."

"I'm not surprised, but as Charity knows, I'm more of a mocha guy," Quinn answered. "I'd love to get a large mocha with whip from Java Café if you can spare Charity for ten minutes."

"But, of course," Sam answered, walking with them to the door. "And if you ever feel like talking about your big spread down on the river, I'm your man. I heard through the grapevine that you've been toying with the idea of selling it. I specialize in handling the more exclusive Paradise Valley properties. Affluent people on the East and West Coasts all seem to want a piece of Montana these days."

"All the better reason to keep them out of our valley." Quinn smiled and tipped his head. "Let's go get that mocha, Charity."

CHARITY WAS STILL in shock as she stepped out of the office with Douglas—Quinn.

She shot him a bewildered glance as they reached the curb. "I don't know what to say," she said huskily, bundling her arms across her chest as they crossed the street, heading for Java Café.

Quinn took off his coat and draped it over her shoulders.

"That's not necessary," she protested.

"You were cold."

"What about you?"

"I'm a man."

She snorted on muffled laughter and then gave her head a shake. "What are you doing here?"

"I came to see you."

"Why?"

"Because that's what friends do. They stay in touch." Quinn's voice was even, almost careless as he asked, "Is that the Greg you dated?"

She shot him another, equally uneasy side glance. "Yes."

"He's even worse than you said."

She fought a slightly hysterical bubble of laughter, as she

tugged the coat closer. "You were never supposed to meet him. I was never supposed to see you again. I confided in Douglas Quincy, not Quinn Douglas, so Quinn Douglas should be very careful about commenting on my personal life."

"You have a little bit of fire in you."

"Listen, I know you're a big deal to a lot of people here, but I'm uncomfortable you know so much about me, and I'm sorry I told you so much about myself at Little Teton. It was a mistake—"

"I'm still your friend, Charity."

"No, you were Tricia's friend. Not mine."

He reached past her to open the door to Java Café. "Tricia doesn't have two sisters named Jenny and Mandy. Tricia didn't date a guy named Greg that loves the Cubs. Tricia doesn't love to sketch—"

"Okay, I did tell you about me," she said quietly, urgently, aware that others were looking at them and people were beginning to recognize Quinn. "We hung out for five days, four nights and we talked about everything, but that's because neither of us had anything to lose. It was confessional. Good for the soul."

"So why are you upset then?" He asked, steering her toward the Christmas tree in the corner, and then turning his back on the café.

"Because you're not this writer from the Pacific Northwest. You're Quinn Douglas from Marietta. You're someone *famous*. You're that guy that everyone wants." Her voice cracked. "You're some superstar and I'm just… *me*. And let's face it, I'm in a not-so-great place, having to work daily with a horrible guy, while my sister wants me to come work for her, and I can't do it because, even though I love her, I would hate having to stand at the front desk of her pink hair salon answering the phone and greeting everyone. It sounds awful. Smiling, smiling, smiling… being cheerful and friendly to every person that walks in the door." She shuddered. "It's one thing to do that at an insurance office, and then at Melk, but at your little sister's hair salon? No, thank you."

"So don't work for your sister. And don't work for Melk. Do what you want to do."

"I can't make a living as a fashion designer."

"Well, you haven't exactly tried."

Her jaw tightened, temper stirred. "Now that's not fair."

"I'm simply saying if being a designer is what you really want, you would have taken steps to make your dream a reality."

"This is why I regret sharing. I told you things thinking I would never have to see you again, but you are here, and you know my worst darkest secrets, and to add insult to injury, you're flinging them at me."

"I wouldn't say flinging."

She nearly stomped her foot. "What happened to you? Where did Douglas Quincy go? I liked him a lot better."

"I'm one and the same."

"That's what Tricia said, but you're not a sportswriter."

"I used to have a sports blog, but I've recently switched to a podcast."

"What can't you do?"

"Sew. Sketch. Design."

She turned her head away, frustrated. "I'm not mad at you," she said after a long, tense moment. "I'm just embarrassed."

"Why?"

"Everyone in this town knows who you are but me."

"I like that you didn't know."

"Why?"

"Because I like that you liked me for me. That means a lot to me." He gave her a crooked smile. "So a mocha?"

She nodded, feeling forlorn.

"With whip?" he asked.

She nodded again, and then watched him walk to the counter, all gorgeous male swagger.

Her heart thumped and her chest squeezed tight, aware that almost everyone in Java Café was watching him, too.

Quinn Douglas wasn't just any handsome man, nor was he just any professional athlete. He was Marietta's own. He mattered to so many.

Quinn returned a few minutes later with their coffees. "You look like you're about to bolt."

Her pulse was hammering and everything in her wanted

to run. "You can read me pretty well."

"What's going on in your head?"

What was going on? She liked him. *A lot.* But he was so out of her league, and the fact that he was so out of her league made her want to throw up. "Too much. I'm pretty overwhelmed."

"You're just having coffee with a friend."

She glanced out the window, toward her office building on the other side of the street. She could have sworn someone was at the window of her office—Sam? Greg? It didn't really matter. Sam didn't care if she took a half hour off for coffee. In fact, he wouldn't care if she took the rest of the day off if he thought that would help him get Quinn's business. "Let's sit," she said.

"Good idea. These cups are hot."

The corner booth near the window was free and she slid into the narrow wooden seat, and then he sat down on the wooden bench adjacent to hers. The table was so small Quinn's knees brushed hers before he shifted his legs away, but that one brief touch was enough to make her insides flip and her pulse hum. She hadn't stopped thinking about their kiss since it happened. It was without a doubt, the best kiss of her life.

Driving back from Wyoming, she'd told herself to savor it because it was special. It was a once-in-a-lifetime kiss. And yet now Mr. Once-in-a-Lifetime was sitting here, across from her, at Java Café. Mr. Once-in-a-Lifetime was Marietta's favorite hero.

"How is your mocha?" Quinn asked politely.

"Delicious," she answered, taking another sip from her mocha and waiting to see what he'd say next, determined to leave conversation to him. At Little Teton, they'd sat with each other plenty of times without speaking, and Charity had never been uncomfortable then. It was different now. *They* were different now.

Seconds went by. A minute. And still he said nothing. The silence was maddening.

"What are you thinking?" she finally blurted.

"I'm trying to figure out what has you so scared."

"I just feel… naked."

"You're not."

"I'm worried about all the things I told you, things that are deeply personal and I thought in that moment I shared it was okay, because the information was contained. No one would know, and when you returned to Seattle, you'd forget all about me, but here we are, in my favorite coffee place in Marietta, and I'm pretty sure you remember everything I told you."

"Of course."

"So you can see why I feel as if my 'sharing' was a mistake?"

"I was open, too. I shared about Alice and my relationship, because that's what people do."

"Alice didn't treat you badly, though. Greg was pretty

awful. I didn't realize you'd actually meet him one day."

"I'd love five minutes in a boxing ring with him—"

"No!"

"He doesn't belong in this town. We don't treat women badly in this town."

"But that's what I mean. I've had really different experiences here in Marietta than you have. People do love you, Quinn. People don't love the Wrights. We have really different backgrounds, and we come from different families."

"I knew your dad in high school. He wasn't a bad man, Charity."

She hated that Quinn knew about her father's drinking. It had been out of control for years. "We struggled a lot financially. There was a time where we wouldn't have survived if not for the kindness of strangers, as well as the support of local churches and charities." She swallowed around the lump in her throat. "I've always hated my name because it's how we existed. On charity."

"Our ranch in Paradise Valley got by on a wing and a prayer," he answered. "It was badly managed. My dad wasn't cut out to be a rancher. He didn't know the first thing about taking care of the land."

"You're just saying that to make me feel better."

"Talk to Rory. He'll tell you. The ranch was a disaster. My folks were deeply in debt when they died." His brow creased and his jaw hardened. He waited a moment before adding, "There's a reason I own a big house in Paradise

Valley with just a couple acres of land. I want the privacy, without the property. I don't want to graze cattle. I don't want to breed horses. I don't want to wear chaps or play cowboy. I love the valley with the views of the mountains and the river, but I'm not cut out to be a rancher. It's a hard life, especially come winter, and I've known since I was eleven years old that it's not for me."

"So even before the—tragedy—on your place?"

"Yes." His gaze met hers and held. "I've only ever wanted to play ball. I was that kid that slept with his glove. My mom used to throw the ball to me when I was still in diapers. My dad and Rory would be out working somewhere and she'd be at the stove, making dinner, and I'd bring her a ball and beg her to play with me."

Charity's chest felt so terribly tender. "She'd be so proud of what you've done."

He shrugged. "The point is, I don't talk about my mom with just anyone. I rarely mentioned my family to Alice. There was no reason to. But it's different with you. I feel comfortable talking to you, and I think it's because you don't have any expectations of who I'm supposed to be. You just accept me for me."

"So you don't care that my mom took us to the thrift store behind the gun shop to do our back-to-school shopping?"

"No."

"And you don't care that we never bought our own

Thanksgiving turkeys until Jenny had her first job and was able to buy it for us herself?"

"No."

She glanced down at her cup and noted the pale pink smudge from her lipstick on the rim. She rubbed at the mark. It faded but couldn't be completely erased. "Okay," she said softly.

"Okay?"

She lifted her head and looked at him, her chest still overly tight. He'd impressed her as the handsome, charming sportswriter Douglas Quincy, but as tough, uncompromising Quinn Douglas, he absolutely touched her heart.

"Well?" he prompted quietly. "What do you think?"

She wanted to reach out to him, to slip her hand into his. She wanted contact and connection and closeness, but those things created risk. She wanted him in her world, without the risk. "We can do this," she said. "I'd like to still be friends."

"I'm glad to hear it."

"But I worry about something."

He leaned forward, closing the distance between them. "I'm listening."

And he was. His blue gaze focused intently on her mouth, and his expression was attentive. He was so close she could see flecks of silver in his blue eyes and the fine lines at the corner of his eyes. His skin was still lightly tan, revealing all the hours he spent out in the sun. Her finger itched to trace the light creases and his dense black lashes.

"I could use a friend like you," she said carefully. "But Quinn, this is such a small world."

"I know."

"People will get involved. They'll say things. They'll judge."

"You mean Carol Bingley and her crew might gossip, but Sadie won't ever gossip or judge, and your sister won't, and my sister won't, either. They all love you, and they respect you, and conveniently, they all respect me."

She couldn't look away from his lovely face. It astonished her that in just days he'd become familiar and dear. "You have friends. You have fans—thousands and thousands of them. Let's be honest, you don't need me in your life—"

"Are you for real?" he demanded, jaw flexing.

Her face burned, and she dropped her gaze. "I'm trying to be honest, and practical. I think being honest is essential, which is why I want you to agree that the moment this... friendship... is a burden or a hassle, in any way, we let it go."

"Friends don't drop friends because one is a burden or a hassle. Furthermore, I can't imagine you would ever be a burden or a hassle. That's Greg the Schmuck filling your head with nonsense. I want you on my team. I picked you for my team. I'm not letting you go."

"I've never really been on a team, other than with my sister."

"I have. I've spent my life on teams, and the best teams,

the most successful teams work together, stick together, and look out for each other."

"Got it," she said.

"Good. Now join us for dinner tonight. McKenna has booked a big table at Rocco's. McKenna and Trey, Sadie and Rory, with their four hundred kids—"

She laughed at that, her snort not muffled enough.

His hands lifted. "Okay, there aren't four hundred. There are only three I know of, but it can feel like four hundred when they all start crying at the same time." His smile warmed. "Come on. Join us. McKenna and Sadie would love to have you there. They're your friends. We're all your friends."

She was tempted by the invitation, so tempted, but she'd already made plans with her sister for tonight and maybe it was for the best, as her feelings for Quinn were far stronger than she'd first imagined, and strong feelings were dangerous, because they weren't in a romantic relationship.

"I wish I could," she said, "but Mandy and I have planned a girls' night in for tonight. After work, we're meeting for pizza and a glass of wine."

"I'm glad. I know you've missed her."

And yet she already regretted turning him down for tonight. She would have enjoyed dinner with him and his family. "Maybe another time before you leave? When do you leave?"

"I have a flight out of Bozeman tomorrow."

"Oh." Her heart sank. "I see. When do you think you'll return?"

"I'm hoping to be back for Christmas."

That was only a couple weeks away. "Stay for a few days when you come back. We can see a movie or go skating at Miracle Lake."

"Perfect." He pulled out his phone. "Give me your number."

"My number?"

"Friends keep in touch through calls and texts."

She blushed. "Right." She rattled off her number and watched him save it. "I better get back to work." Charity returned his coat to him and then leaned over to give a quick, awkward hug. "Stay in touch."

"You, too."

"I don't have your number."

"I've already texted it to you."

AMANDA'S HAIR SALON, The Wright Salon, was in an older house that had been painted pink and it looked festive with all its boughs of greenery.

A sole stylist was still working downstairs at her station in what had once been the living room. Amanda waved Charity to come to what had been the dining room and was now a pretty sitting room for clients in between appointments.

Amanda had the bottle of wine open and two glasses on the table. "Pizza is coming," she said, dropping into a white slipcovered armchair. "Ah, this feels good to sit. It was busy today."

Charity curled into the corner of the couch, tucking her legs under her. "It was a busy day," she agreed. "Not sure if you heard…"

"I heard." Grinning, Amanda leaned forward to fill their two glasses. "Quinn Douglas, my sweet Charity. Now there's a catch. Marietta's most eligible bachelor. Earns millions every year—"

"I could care less about the money."

"Comes from a great family. We all adore McKenna."

"I'm not dating him, Amanda. He and I have agreed to be friends."

"That's a good first step."

"I'm serious. It's not romantic."

"But he's perfect for you."

"He's not perfect for me. He's perfect for a perfect woman. I'm not her."

"So, is that what this is about? Your poor self-esteem?"

"I'm tired, Mandy. I'm not in the mood to be analyzed."

"You're the one keeping you from happy-ever-after—" Amanda broke off at the sound of the doorbell. "Hold that thought. We're not done here."

Charity shifted miserably on the couch while Amanda retrieved the pizza, not wanting to discuss Quinn anymore with her sister, or anyone.

Amanda came sailing back into the sitting room and placed the pizza and plates and napkins on the coffee table in front of them. "No one is perfect," she said, opening the box and placing two slices of pizza on each of their plates. "Quinn's not perfect. I never implied he was. I said he was perfect for you."

"Mandy, I know how this will play out, and I can't handle more disappointment. Not right now."

"Loser Greg hurt you that much?"

Charity started to lift a pizza slice and set it back down. "Or maybe Loser Charity hurt me this much, because I've done an excellent job of making bad decisions. And, yes, I do feel banged up. I feel stupid and bruised. It seems I'm lousy at reading people... specifically guys... and I don't want to keep making mistakes."

"Well, I'm pretty good at reading people, and I'd say your only real problem is a lack of confidence, which is why you've been dating the wrong guys for the past couple of years."

"I used to be better at this," Charity said quietly. "Once upon a time there was Joe."

"And you were crazy about him."

"I was."

"But you hated that his ranch was so remote."

"It was. You've been there. It's way up on the mountain—and windy and bitterly cold."

Amanda simply smiled as she bit into her pizza.

Charity saw her sister's smile. "*What?*"

Amanda just chewed and shrugged her shoulders.

"You never liked him," Charity said irritably.

Amanda blotted her mouth on a paper napkin and then wiped her fingers. "I didn't dislike him, but I thought it was wrong of him to not meet you part way. His ranch is remote, but it wasn't just his ranch that scared you. He lived with his grandfather and mother and four brothers and you would have become a cook and housekeeper to all of them. It wasn't going to be a paradise for you. You were going to be isolated and lonely and he didn't get it. He didn't want to see how life would change for you. It was all about him, and what he needed, and, let's face it, Joe wasn't the kind of guy who'd let you drive on your own to town every day, especially in winter. He's so old-fashioned and protective, he'd say, *'Wait babe, I'll drive you on Saturday when I'm done working.'*" Amanda's eyebrows rose. "That's what terrified you. Being trapped out there and not having any friends close by."

Charity chewed her bite slowly, her heart heavy, because Amanda was right. Charity needed people, and town, and activity. Joe had grown up on his family property, and the only life he knew was the life of a cowboy and rancher, and he didn't understand her fear, or her need to remain close to her sister. Their big fight and breakup was about Mandy, too. He'd said she was too dependent on her sister, and that dependence wasn't good for her. His words had wounded, and infuriated her. How dare he criticize her for being close with her sister, when he still lived and worked with his brothers? How dare he say she was too dependent when he wasn't having to give up anything? She was the one who'd lose her world, not him.

And so they fought, hard, with the same passion they'd once loved each other, and neither of them would back down. Neither would apologize nor compromise. One day became a week, and then a week became a month, and months turned into a year.

A year after they broke up, she heard he was engaged to another girl, and Charity was privately devastated. She told no one that she was upset, not even her sister, but it had hurt her terribly that he could just move on so easily without her.

She forced herself to move on and began dating here and there. The dates were all vaguely depressing. None of the men were Joe. None had his quiet intensity, or his rugged masculinity, or his beautiful face and shaggy dark blond hair and piercing blue eyes—

Dark blond hair, piercing blue eyes, beautiful face.

Charity dropped her pizza slice and reached for a napkin. She wiped her fingers and then balled it in her hand. "They kind of look alike," she said in a low, strangled voice.

"The Wyatt brothers? Of course—"

"*No.* Quinn and Joe. They both have the same look... the same sexy rugged I-can-do-anything look."

"Oh, you mean hot alpha look." Amanda's eyebrows arched. "You've always like alphas far more than I did."

"Tyler is not a beta hero."

"No. But he's not the Tarzan, beat-on-your-chest kind of guy that appeals to you."

"That's true. I do like the muscles and wickedly handsome."

"So to recap, you don't like Quinn because he resembles Joe, because they look nothing alike. Joe's hair was brown and his eyes were green, and Quinn has dark blond hair—"

"I know what Quinn looks like," Charity interrupted testily.

"You like Quinn because he makes you feel safe, and protected, like Joe did."

Charity mulled this over for a moment. "Quinn does make me feel good," she admitted.

"I think you should give Quinn a chance when he returns for Christmas."

"He comes back almost every year." Amanda reached for the bottle of wine and topped off each of their glasses. "And when he's back, give him a chance. It's silly to impose these rules—"

"I'm not imposing rules."

"Forcing him into the friend zone is all about control and rules."

"Maybe I don't want this with Quinn to blow up. He is a seriously nice guy."

"And hot, and sexy, and successful, and financially stable."

"I don't care about money, so please stop talking about his portfolio."

Amanda laughed, and then her smile faded. "He's not too good for you. If anything, he's not good enough for you, Charity. You are one of the best human beings I know."

For a long moment, there was just silence, and the silence made Charity incredibly uncomfortable. She gulped her wine and deliberately changed the topic. "So tell me about the Stroll. How was it this year? Did I miss anything?"

AN HOUR AND a half later, Charity quietly let herself into her parents' house on Chance Avenue. The house was small and square and painted a faded blue. Charity and Mandy had tried to repaint it but their mom and dad apparently like the shade and didn't want them to spend even twenty dollars on a couple cans of paint to freshen up the trim, so the house remained as it had been for years—blue and unbearably forlorn.

Charity discovered her mom was still up watching TV, so she gave her a hug and said good night and was about to slip to her room when her mother asked about Amanda, and how she and Tyler were doing.

"Good," Charity answered vaguely, feeling guilty they hadn't discussed Amanda and Tyler's relationship very much, but Amanda seemed happy—as well as determined to get Charity set up with Quinn. "Mandy seems happy. Work has been busy and her day spa is getting great reviews. She has picked up new business with her new masseuse."

"Any mention of babies?"

Charity rolled her eyes. "No, Mom. But it hasn't even been six months since they married. Give them time. I'd think they'd want a couple years just to enjoy being together before kids come along."

"I had Jenny right away."

"You married Dad because Jenny was on the way, and you and Dad were stressed out of your minds. No one else wants that life."

"We were happy," her mom answered defensively. She must have noticed the arch in Charity's brows. "We did the best we could."

"I know that. We all know that. But if Mandy and Tyler want to wait five years, or ten years, before having children, then they should. The point of falling in love isn't to imme- diately reproduce. It's to make a life with your best friend—" Charity broke off, aware of what she'd just said.

A life with your best friend.

Your *friend.*

Immediately, her thoughts went to Quinn and then she shied away.

"What were you saying?" her mother asked, smothering a yawn. "You didn't finish your thought."

"Nothing important," Charity answered. "I'm heading to bed. I have an early morning meeting so I'll be up and gone early."

"For work?"

"No. It's the Christmas tree auction."

"Again?"

"We meet weekly, Mom, and it's coming up in just ten days."

"Is Mandy helping this year?"

"She's not on the committee but Sadie convinced her to donate a tree."

"Let me guess, it's pink?"

"You know your baby girl." Charity returned to her mother to give her a quick kiss on the cheek. "Good night, and don't stay up half the night watching TV. Even you, Mom, need sleep."

CHAPTER FIVE

AFTER DINNER AT Rocco's, Quinn returned to his house in Paradise Valley. When he'd left for dinner, the dozens of west-facing windows reflected the setting sun, the glass glazed with pink and red light. Now it was dark, clouds obscuring the moon, blanketing the valley in darkness.

Fortunately, he'd left on a light in the kitchen and the house glowed yellow as he parked in the driveway. He sat for a moment, engine idling, looking at the front exterior with the big beam trusses, long covered porch, and river rock chimneys. It was handsome and expensive, but far from festive. A different owner would have put lights up by now, and added greenery to the mantel, candles on tables, and a towering Christmas tree in the great room. A different owner would know how to make the house homey.

A family would also make this house homey. Baking in the kitchen. High chairs at the island. Kids with toys and noise and small plush blankets forgotten on the stairs.

Quinn thought of Charity, and pictured her here, blonde hair in a ponytail as she stirred something at the stove, before crossing to the kitchen's gas fire and flicking the switch, making the huge hearth glow.

She was what this house needed. She was what he needed. She was sweet and warm, and incredibly down-to-earth.
She was also heartbreakingly pretty but by far the best thing
about her was her smile. When she smiled, her eyes shone,
her lips curved, her face softened. It would be so easy to fall
in love with her. He was already smitten. More than smitten.
He hadn't been able to stop thinking about her since she left
Little Teton, and seeing her today just confirmed his feelings. She was his. He just needed time to convince her that
she belonged with him, and until then, he needed to keep
other men away.

Quinn stepped from his truck and was in the middle of
unlocking the front door when his phone rang. For a split
second he wondered—*hoped, actually*—it might be Charity.

Instead it was Alice, and as he closed the front door, his
spark of enthusiasm faded.

"Hi, Alice. What's up?"

"I haven't heard from you since you arrived in Wyoming. Just wondered how the week went."

Quinn peeled off his coat and dropped his keys on the
kitchen island. "It was good. I was impressed by Little
Teton."

"You're going to invest."

"I haven't decided."

"You know Dad wants it."

Of course Leo did. Anytime Leo smelled blood, he'd

rush in for the kill. "Peter hasn't decided to sell it," Quinn answered carelessly, deciding then and there to cut Peter a check so he didn't have to deal with Sterling Enterprises salivating at Peter's doorstep.

"We'll see. You know my dad, and he usually gets what he wants."

"Oh, I know."

She paused. "He's invited you to join us for Christmas. It'll be another white Christmas at the Jackson Hole house. Please come. It won't be Christmas without you."

"I'm going to be spending Christmas this year in Marietta with family."

"You say that every year."

"I've just confirmed my plans with my sister. I'm not going to disappoint McKenna."

"Marietta isn't half as fun as Jackson Hole."

"Marietta is really charming, especially in December. Ice skating, gingerbread competition, caroling on Main Street."

"You make it sound like a Hallmark movie," she said, and from her tone it wasn't a compliment. "Nothing is that cute."

"It's pretty cute right now and it's not even Christmas."

"You're in Montana?"

"Arrived today, but I'm on a flight out of Bozeman tomorrow."

"Want me to pick you up at the airport?"

"Thank you for offering," he said politely, "but my car's

there."

"Oh."

He held his breath, certain her next question would be a suggestion that they meet for dinner, or grab drinks at Canon. "Listen, Alice, I hope you've begun dating again. You should be. You're a beautiful woman—"

"I miss you, Quinn."

"Sweetheart, we're not going to get back together."

"We were good together!"

"I don't think we were, not really. We stayed together because it was just easier than going through a breakup and having to start fresh."

"That's not true. I love you, and I know you loved me."

"I will always care for you, but we weren't a good fit. We weren't even that compatible. I like your dad, and he was always kind to me, but I couldn't ever work for him, and Seattle isn't my home. Montana is. This is where I want to raise my kids. This is who I am."

"I know I got upset that time about Montana, but I've thought a lot about it and there is no reason we couldn't go back and forth. The kids would of course go to school in Seattle, but we could summer in Montana, even though summer is the nicest time of year here and I love our house on Vashon—"

"Alice, any kids I have, will go to school here."

"Baby, you went to elementary school in a one-room schoolhouse."

"I did. And it was fantastic."

"That's not the education kids need today to get into top colleges. It's competitive out there. They need the best schools, and I appreciate you were a great athlete, so that helped you, but I don't want my kids spending valuable learning time being taught how to hunt and fish and whatever else they taught you."

"Reading, writing, math, history, science."

"History meaning, Montana history."

Quinn rubbed his temple, trying to rub away the ache. It seemed like every other call with her ended like this. She wouldn't let him go and yet she didn't want what he wanted. She wanted him, without wanting the true him. "I don't want to do this anymore," he said quietly. "I can't do this anymore. You need to let go and move forward. I am."

Her voice was muffled when she spoke again. "You're dating other people?"

He paused before answering, "There is someone."

"Is it serious?"

"I like her, and that's all I'm going to say."

"Where does she live?"

"Alice, we're not going to discuss it."

"Is she in Montana?"

"Take care of yourself. Try to be happy. Goodbye." And then he hung up and turned his phone off to keep from having to deal with frantic calls from Alice because he knew how it'd go. She'd call back teary and desperate, and then she'd become angry and bitter, and he hated conflict, and hated the fights. Alice had perfected arguing.

His good mood gone, Quinn turned the TV on in the great room to *Sports Channel* but he was too keyed up to sit. Instead, he returned to the kitchen and filled a glass with water and then wandered around downstairs as the broadcasters talked about highlights from tonight's NBA games.

Despite being unoccupied most of the time, the house was spotless. His weekly housekeeping service made sure there was never dust. Surfaces gleamed. The creamy marble kitchen countertops were an elegant contrast to the handsome split-log walls. During the day, the huge windows in the great room brought the rugged Montana landscape in. This afternoon, the Gallatin Range, dominated by Copper Mountain, had been blanketed in white, but now all beyond his window was dark.

He liked this house. He wanted to love it. He didn't. At least, not yet. One day maybe he would.

Maybe when he was done playing ball he could live here and make it a real home. He wasn't ready to give up ball, though. He'd had a great season last year and he felt strong, and healthy, and more players were playing longer. Why couldn't he?

He'd loved baseball since he was a little kid, and he'd wanted to play professionally for as long as he could remember. When he was finally drafted out of University of Washington where he'd gone on a full sports scholarship, he'd vowed to be the best professional baseball player possible, and he'd honored that vow by training hard, getting rest, avoiding the party scene, as well as the groupies.

He was a monogamist, and when the single guys flirted with women in the hotel lobby, he headed up to his room, and called Alice. Before Alice, he'd been with Heather for four years, and before Heather, it had been Dominique for two.

Unlike his brother Rory, who'd always been a tortured lone wolf, Quinn valued the pack. Quinn wanted his own partner, and he looked forward to children, and he was ready for children... babies. At thirty-seven, he was mature and financially sound, and the only reason he wasn't a dad already was that he hadn't found the right woman.

Leaning on the marble island, his gaze swept the rich wood kitchen cabinetry and the long wood table and chairs in the adjacent dining room. The table seated twelve comfortably. Clearly, when he built this house, he hadn't planned on being single so long.

Once again his thoughts returned to Charity and then he gave his head a shake, stopping himself from going there.

She wasn't ready, and he still had ball. How could he pursue her from Seattle? How could he prove to her he was the right one when he lived so far away? The logistics were problematic. She loved Marietta. She'd made that clear. Could he convince her to come out and visit him in Seattle? Or was it just too much, too soon?

IT WAS A cold blustery morning and Charity arrived at Main Street Diner with her teeth chattering, desperate for that first hot cup of coffee.

There were five of them at the meeting and the mood was mostly buoyant as nearly all of the tickets had been sold and they spent their hour together ironing out final details and making sure they had sufficient silent auction items. Everyone agreed to try to round up one to two more silent auction items each, and then Sadie Douglas the cochair for this year's auction discussed the dinner and dancing portion, before Risa Scott, the other cochair discussed the setup and decorations, and then the meeting was over.

It was refreshing to leave Main Street Diner feeling good about the event, and everything they'd accomplished to even reach this point, especially considering the auction was still a new thing in Marietta. The Christmas Tree Gala, Mistletoe and Montana, used to be a Livingston event but when Marietta's Graff Hotel proved to be a better venue, Marietta embraced the fund-raiser and it had become even more successful. This year, Gallagher Tree Farm was the event's biggest sponsor, and their early donation had made planning and execution so much easier.

Charity returned to her car, and drove to the small parking lot behind her office building. As she walked around to the front entrance on Main, she spotted a big golden retriever walking down the street. The dog's head and tail drooped.

Periodically the dog would stop, and sniff a patch of snow, and then continue on.

She stopped to watch him, wondering if he was looking for food or trying to track his human. She hoped he wasn't lost, or abandoned. It was unusual to see dogs loose on Main Street. In fact, the city would have someone out to take him to an animal shelter if he lingered downtown too long.

She watched a moment longer before going into the office. Sam was already there before her, at work at his desk. She checked the coffeepot. Coffee was brewing. She stuck her head into Sam's office and asked if he needed anything.

"No, I'm good," he answered. "Just as an FYI, I have some people flying in from San Francisco, interested in buying property in Paradise Valley. They land mid morning and I'll be picking them up and then expect to be out of the office the rest of the day."

"Do you have some good leads to show them?"

"Actually, no. There is nothing on the market right now that exactly meets their needs. They don't really want acreage. They want a big house on Yellowstone River with a dynamite view of the Gallatin's." He paused and gave her a meaningful look. "Like Quinn Douglas's place. I don't suppose he'd want to sell it?"

"We've never talked about his house," she answered.

"He spent a fortune on it and yet he's maybe stayed there a half-dozen times."

She shrugged. "It's his house."

"Yeah, but it's a lot of money—millions of dollars—and he doesn't seem to really enjoy it. I'm tempted to follow up with him about his place. Actually, I'm tempted to just send you to talk to him about selling it."

"Send me where? To Seattle?"

"As of this morning, Quinn's still in town."

"Maybe for coffee, but he's flying out of Bozeman this morning."

"He was. There's been an accident over at the Gallagher Tree Farm and I've been told he's gone there to help."

"What happened?"

"I don't know that yet."

Charity went to her desk and turned her computer on but couldn't focus on her email inbox. What happened at the Gallaghers? Who'd been hurt?

She glanced at her watch. It was only just eight now. Whatever happened, happened early. She sat there stewing, and was still stewing when she looked up and spotted the golden retriever outside in front of the real estate office.

He looked forlorn. Her heart went out to him.

Charity left her desk and returned to Sam's office. He was on the phone but he held his finger up, signaling he wanted her to wait. She did. He finished the call a few moments later.

"That was my sister, Kerry," he said. "Sawyer is being prepped for surgery now. His leg looked pretty bad. Jenna, Sawyer's wife is with him."

Kerry was a nurse that worked part-time at Marietta Medical so she'd have accurate information. "At least Jenna is there with him."

"Jenna is having problems, though. She's having contractions. They're discussing admitting her because they don't want the baby to arrive just yet."

"Oh, no!"

"Thankfully Quinn is over at the Gallagher's place now. He got there before the ambulance arrived and helped Jenna extract Sawyer from the baler."

"That's how he got hurt?"

"One of Sawyer's guys wasn't paying attention and Sawyer stepped in, saving him."

"Only now Sawyer's hurt," she said in a small voice.

"I have to think he's going to be off of his feet for the next few weeks."

"They can't afford to operate without him. It's a family business."

"There is good news, though."

"Oh?"

"Looks like your Quinn Douglas will be sticking around now."

Charity rolled her eyes and started for her desk, glancing out the big glass window to the street, and there out front was the golden retriever, sitting on the curb, head cocked.

The dog!

She returned to Sam's office door for a third time. "Sorry. I knew there was something I wanted to ask you. Do you know anyone with a golden retriever?"

He'd started to make another call and he briefly glanced up from his phone. "Some of the folks near me have Labs, a chocolate Lab and a blonde Lab. But I don't know anyone with a retriever. Why?"

"There's a beautiful one outside. He's been on the street ever since I arrived."

"Somebody will claim him."

"I don't want him to get hurt."

"He won't."

"I'll see if he has a collar on, or any tags. Maybe there is someone I can call."

She grabbed her coat and stuffed her arms into the sleeves before stepping outside. But just as she approached the dog, a car pulled into the empty parking spot out front and honked the horn, loudly, scaring the dog away.

It was Greg. Of course.

She shook her head, disgusted. Why honk at the dog? What purpose was there in doing such a thing?

Charity ignored Greg as he entered the real estate office, focusing instead on getting through her emails. But Greg stopped at her desk, and just stood there without saying a word, and continued to stand there, staring down at her in silence, for at least a minute.

He was so annoying. She ground her teeth together and bit her tongue. Finally, fed up, she looked upward. "Can I help you?"

"You could sound a little more friendly."

"Why? We're not friends."

"You're supposed to be professional."

"So are you. Please move along to your own desk. This is mine."

"Don't make me tell Sam that we can't work together," he said. "I'd hate to see you lose your job."

She battled her temper, and then her temper won. "You mean you would love it. New receptionist here means new meat for you."

"I'm a good guy."

"Just keep telling yourself that."

Greg bent down, leaning closer. "It doesn't have to be this way. There's no reason for so much animosity."

Indignation flooded her. She lifted a hand to keep him from coming any closer. "A little personal space, please."

He muttered something uncomplimentary and then stalked off. Charity forced her attention back to her computer but her hands were shaking as she tried to type and she found it hard to focus. Greg was awful. She hated having to work with him. She went to bed dreading work, and woke up even more miserable. She couldn't afford to quit now, just before the holidays, but it was definitely time to look for a new job. Maybe working for her sister wouldn't be that bad.

Or maybe pursuing design and custom work wouldn't be

bad either.

The little voice in her head made her catch her breath. Ever since she'd met Quinn, that little voice had been pretty talkative, and it was loud right now.

Why not pursue her dreams? Why had she given up on them?

She'd always had a flare for fashion, and she loved making gorgeous clothes... perhaps it wasn't ridiculous to become Marietta's first fashion designer. It wasn't as if she had to leave Marietta to do it, and she didn't need much to get started, as she already had her sewing machines and embroidery machines and everything else required. The key thing would be getting the word out, and letting people know she was taking custom orders. The local bridal shop, Married in Marietta, could carry some of her evening wear, and maybe one day, she could even have her own shop downtown to display her designs.

Her friends here had their own businesses. McKenna was a photographer and worked out of her home. Sadie had her shabby chic business on Main Street. Her sister, Amanda, had started small, working for someone else on Main Street, before opening her own salon two years ago. If they could do it, she could. She just had to be confident, and wouldn't it be fun to prove the naysayers wrong?

After replying to a couple of emails requiring immediate attention, Charity put in a call to Sadie, who was also married to Rory, Quinn's brother.

"Sam told me about the accident at the Gallagher Tree Farm," Charity said when Sadie answered. "I understand that Sawyer is in surgery and Jenna's having contractions?"

"I just talked to Jenna," Sadie said. "The contractions have stopped. She and the baby are fine, but they're keeping her overnight for observation."

"So both of them will be at the hospital tonight?"

"It sounds like it, but she's hoping they'll both be allowed to return home tomorrow. She knows Sawyer will be anxious about needing to get back to work, but it's the same leg he broke a couple years ago. ER called in Wyatt Gallagher—the orthopedist, not related to the tree farm Gallaghers—to do the surgery and he's one of the best in the county. Sawyer should be fine in the long run."

THE EARLY MORNING chaos had calmed down enough at the Gallagher Christmas Tree Farm for Quinn to take a tour of the premises and figure out what he needed to do.

He was also craving a cup of coffee as he hadn't had one yet today. Normally he had a cup before breakfast but today he'd been woken up by a call from his sister, alerting him to an accident that had just taken place at the Gallaghers. McKenna said an ambulance was on the way but he was the closest person she knew to the Gallagher property and help was needed there, fast.

Quinn knew how important neighbors were in the

ranching community and he threw on clothes and headed straight over. Quinn used to play ball with Sawyer when they were kids, and the boys from Paradise Valley would always carpool together. Because Sawyer was closer to town, he was always the first to be dropped off, and the last to be picked up. The Gallaghers' tree farm had been in their family for generations, with their land butting up against the national forest on the lower slopes of Copper Mountain.

It felt good to see the old wooden sign pointing to the farm. That meant he was almost there. Not long after, he pulled into the gravel parking lot. To the right was the barn, and in between were dozens of trees, some up in stands, others on the ground.

A tall, thin man in a baseball cap ran toward Quinn as he climbed from the truck. "I've got Sawyer's leg out of the baler but it's broken. There's blood everywhere. You can see a bone sticking out," the man said.

Quinn had seen some bad breaks in baseball and he knew the basics for a compound fracture—stop the bleeding, splint, and wrap with tape or gauze.

Reaching the cluster of people near the barn, he spotted Sawyer on a wool blanket on the ground and a woman kneeling next to him, holding his hand.

Quinn crouched at his side, his gaze skimming Sawyer's leg with the tattered cord trousers matted with blood. "Hey, bud," he said, giving Sawyer a smile. "How is it going?"

"Mr. Baseball," Sawyer drawled, managing a sickly smile.

"Next time you want an autograph, just give me a call. Happy to drop one off. No need for theatrics." Quinn glanced at Sawyer's wife. "Hi, Jenna. I'm Quinn. My sister thinks the world of you."

"The feeling is reciprocated." Jenna's head lifted. Her eyes were pink and shiny. "His leg doesn't look good."

Quinn carefully rolled up the trouser leg, and she was right. It didn't look good. He was going to need some TLC at the hospital. "The ambulance should be here soon, but in case there's a holdup, I need to slow the bleeding and get a splint on him. I need gauze, tape, and two pieces of wood, shouldn't be hard to find here at a tree farm."

"I've got the first aid kit from the barn," Jenna said.

"I'll get the wood," the man in the baseball cap said.

Sawyer groaned as Quinn gently pulled the tattered fabric from the wound. Jenna blinked hard. "Where is that ambulance?" she whispered huskily, clearly panicked.

"It'll come," Quinn reassured her.

She bit her lip and grimaced, her hand going to her prominent belly. "I think the baby wants to come, too."

"What?" Sawyer tried to sit up. "Are you having contractions?"

"Something's going on." She glanced at Quinn. "Baby Gallagher isn't supposed to arrive until late January."

"Tell the baby to wait," Sawyer ordered. "Dad says so."

In the distance, the wail of a siren could be heard.

"Thank God," Jenna muttered.

Quinn added his own prayer. He'd been prepared to splint Sawyer's leg, but this was much better.

It wasn't until the shrieking ambulance was gone that Quinn turned to the man in the baseball cap. "So what happened here?"

"Crazy accident. I lost my footing and Sawyer moved quick to help me, and then he got hurt."

Quinn studied the guy for a moment. "Can I be straight with you?"

The man hesitated then nodded.

"You smell like booze. I didn't want to say anything in front of the Gallaghers, but have you been drinking?"

The other man took a step back, affronted. "Just a shot to warm me up. We don't have heat at my place right now. Generator's broke."

"Does Sawyer know this?"

"About the generator?"

"That you're struggling."

The man looked uneasy. "I don't want to lose my job."

"Sawyer and I go way back. He wouldn't fire you over being down on your luck, but drinking on the job? That puts not just you, but him, and his entire business at risk." Quinn's arms folded across his chest. "What's your name?"

"Rob Harris."

"Rob, I'm sorry you're having a hard time, but you can't bring that into work. In other words, you can't drink before you come here. You can't drink while here. You can't drink until you get home. So right now, get your things, I'm going to send you home—"

"*What?*"

"Come back tomorrow sober and work hard, and I'll make sure no one docks your wages, but if I ever smell alcohol, or suspect you're drinking while on the job, you're gone, and there won't be another chance."

Rob gave Quinn a long, unhappy look. "I can't go home now. My wife won't understand."

Quinn reached into his back pocket and pulled his wallet out of his jeans. He opened the wallet and extracted two fifty-dollar bills plus a number of twenties and folded them over before handing the wad of bills to Rob. "Tell her you were given the day off to fix the generator. And do it."

Rob glanced down at the money in his hand. "Is this coming from my paycheck?"

"No, it's from me to you, to make sure you can take care of your family. But I expect you to take care of your family, understand?"

"Yes."

"Good. What time do you come? I don't want to keep you waiting tomorrow."

"I'll be here at seven."

"See you then."

After Rob left, Quinn took a walk around the property, inspecting the public areas of the tree farm, from the trees in the stands, to the wreaths stacked on a wooden table, to the big barn overflowing with Christmas lights and decorations. The barn was warm and Christmas music was playing. There was a register at one end and a coffee cart at the other. Quinn lifted one of the big coffee thermoses. It was heavy and sloshed with liquid. Opening the lid steam rose. Hot coffee. Exactly what he needed.

Quinn poured himself a cup, added some sugar and a splash of milk before taking a second walk around the property, studying the pricing on the ornaments and holiday decorations before checking on the register to see how it worked. Petty cash was in the register's till. An iPhone sat next to the register with a little square attached for credit card purchases. He glanced around to see if there was a book for record keeping, or a computer for QuickBooks. He couldn't find one and then thought he'd keep track the old-fashioned way—he'd write each purchase down, and how it was paid for and once Sawyer and Jenna were back, they could sort it out the way they wanted.

Wheels crunched gravel outside and Quinn stepped from the barn with his coffee. He grinned as he saw it was Rory. "What are you doing here?"

"McKenna called me. She thought you might need a hand," Rory said, buttoning up his sheepskin coat and tugging on work gloves.

"There's no one here yet."

"Not right now. But trust me, it's going to get busy."

"Not complaining. It's great to have you here."

"No, Quinn. It's great to have *you* here."

When the first customer arrived a half hour later, Quinn and Rory had divided the labor. For the first part of the morning, Rory was going to bail and load the tree while Quinn rang up purchases, and then they'd switch for the next couple of hours. The system worked, and the day passed quickly. Sadie brought them lunch and stayed to eat with them. She took a peek into the barn to see what decorations they were selling, and then, noticing that coffee was out, she headed into the Gallagher's house to make fresh coffee for the afternoon and returned to work.

By late afternoon traffic picked up significantly. Kids were out of school and families were coming together after work. McKenna's husband, Trey, joined them, and Sadie returned to work the cash register so the guys could all help customers with trees.

Quinn couldn't remember when he'd last enjoyed himself so much. He knew many of the families who stopped in, and even more people recognized him, with quite a few asking for autographs or pictures. He was happy to oblige, and then got the idea that maybe everyone should sign a card for Sawyer, sharing their best wishes.

By five it was dark, and Trey laid a fire in the big fire pit before getting back to work wrapping and anchoring trees onto the waiting line of trucks and cars.

McKenna arrived with the kids and boxes of pizzas. She found the sound system's control and turned on the speakers for the outdoors so Christmas carols played inside the barn and wafted over the tree lot, too.

Quinn hummed along with "God Rest Ye Merry Gentlemen," feeling festive. He liked having his whole family here with him. The only person missing was Charity. And just thinking that thought made him realize how serious he was becoming about her. That was a problem. She wasn't ready for him to have strong feelings. She wasn't ready for anything but friendship. But he'd promised her he'd be there for her, and he would be.

Even if it meant keeping his distance from the one person he wanted to see most.

CHAPTER SIX

CHARITY SPENT THE rest of the day on pins and needles, hoping—expecting—to hear from Quinn. She kept an eye on her phone, even when she went on her lunch and breaks, just in case he texted or called, but he didn't. She told herself he was probably really busy out at the Gallagher Tree Farm, but she kept thinking he might ask her to come out, and do something like Sadie had. This was one of those times that it was hard living in a small town because Charity knew who was out at the tree farm pitching in, and she hadn't been invited. Maybe Sadie wasn't invited, but as Quinn's sister-in-law she could show up when she wanted and stay for as long as she pleased.

Charity drove home after work, and as she made dinner for her parents and herself, she thought she'd happily do a stint at the register. She could restock shelves. Brew coffee, make cookies, basically anything. She'd do it for the Gallaghers—everyone was willing to support the Gallaghers—but her anxiousness was due to Quinn, and not hearing from him.

Why hadn't he sent her at least one text? Why not say

that he'd stayed? Did he think she didn't care, or was he just so busy he forgot about her?

She went to bed feeling rather wistful and woke up even more blue when she discovered still nothing from him. It would have been different if he'd returned to Seattle. She honestly didn't expect to hear much from him once he was back in the Pacific Northwest, but for goodness' sake, he was just down Highway 89. A twenty-minute drive from town!

Once at work, she sent Amanda a text, asking if she'd heard anything about Jenna Gallagher. Had the contractions stopped? Would Jenna and Sawyer be coming home today?

Amanda promised to get info and let Charity know, and then added slyly in a second text, *"You know Quinn is out there working. Maybe you should go pick out a tree?"*

Charity glared at her phone and didn't answer. She settled down to work, and forced herself to ignore her phone and succeeded for nearly an hour when a text popped in from Amanda. *"Just talked to Jenna. She and Sawyer are going home later today. I told Jenna you're bringing a lasagna and garlic bread for dinner. She said Sawyer would be excited. He can't stand hospital food."*

Charity read the message a second time before answering. *"You're a weasel."*

Amanda replied. *"You want to see Quinn. I've given you the opportunity. You can thank me with details later tonight."*

Charity smiled and put her phone away even as Greg appeared in his doorway.

"You're always on that," he said. "Don't you have any

work to do?"

"I'm checking on the Gallaghers."

"If that's what you say."

There was no point in engaging him. Charity returned to the property listing she'd been filling out for Sam. But Greg didn't like being ignored. He crossed to her desk, and cleared off a corner so he could lean on it. "And to think I once thought you were so sweet," he said bitterly. "But you're not. You're cold. You're an ice cube—"

"Right," she said, looking up and giving him a dazzling smile. "I am an ice cube. I'm frigid. Frozen. Brutally cold. Now, is there something you want from me, or are you just going to waste both of our time?"

"I'm not dating Meghan anymore."

She just kept typing.

"It was a mistake," he said. "I'm sorry."

"I accept your apology." She gave him a tight smile. "Now can you go back to your office and find something to do, because I have plenty."

He said something unpleasant under his breath and huffed his way back to his office. Charity watched him a moment and then refused to give him another second of her attention. Before the Wyoming trip she might have dissolved into tears, or at least, felt wounded, but the five days at Little Teton had given her a chance to evaluate her heart. Her heart might have been bruised, but meeting Quinn gave her hope. Nice guys *were* out there. And nice guys *did* like her.

And nice guys kissed *soooo* much better than lame guys.

Her hands hovered over the keyboard as she remembered Quinn's kiss. It had been *amazing*. A little shiver raced through her as she relived the lovely warmth and sensation. She'd left for Wyoming beat-up, and yet she returned to Marietta with energy and excitement and strength.

Charity knew what she looked like—her mom was still pretty, even in her mid-fifties, and her sisters Jenny and Charity were beautiful—but Charity had always been uncomfortable with her looks. It was why she downplayed her appearance whenever possible, pulling her long hair into a ponytail, and keeping her makeup subdued. She needed her value to be based on something other than her face, but apparently that was all Greg had wanted her for. Arm candy.

But arm candy wasn't enough for him. She discovered on Thanksgiving after he'd arrived at Amanda and Tyler's house that there was someone else. She wasn't even looking for trouble, trouble found her when Greg accidentally left his phone on a side table when he went with Tyler to open the red wine.

Greg's phone vibrated, dancing on the wooden table, and then vibrated again. The phone was facing up. Charity glanced down when it vibrated a third time, revealing an incoming pic.

It was a photo of him and a pretty brunette in bed, with a big pink heart around them and the words, *love you, babe*.

Charity had felt sick and she turned the phone over, hiding the image and yet it was seared into her brain.

She was shaking when Greg returned with a glass of wine. Greg didn't even notice she was upset. It was Tyler who asked if everything was alright. She blinked back tears and shook her head.

Greg frowned. "What's happening?" he asked.

She handed him his phone. He looked at it and then turned it off as Tyler discretely left the living room.

"That's not what you think," Greg had said.

She clenched her hands, trying to stay calm. "I'm blonde, not stupid," she said quietly.

"That's an old relationship."

"Is her name Meghan?" she asked, unable to even look at him.

He didn't answer and her eyes burned, and her chest ached, and she felt so unbelievably stupid. "I've heard about her, you know, but I didn't believe it. She lives in Livingston, doesn't she? She's a Pilates instructor. One of my friends saw you take her class and then leave the class with her."

"It was a cardio class."

Charity laughed because she suddenly saw what she'd been trying to ignore. Greg was a liar and a cheat and he'd always been a liar and a cheat and she'd ignored the truth because she was desperate not to be alone. Jenny was gone. Mandy was married. Charity hated having so much time on her hands. But how could she have settled for this? How could she have imagined she was happier with him than on her own?

Her laugh infuriated Greg. "I was never going to marry you," he said. "You're a bimbo looking for a free ride. You just want kids so you can stay home and stop working."

"Because kids aren't work?"

"Men are the breadwinners—"

"Go. Please. Now. Before I get sick." She went to the front door and opened it.

He left without a word but the look he gave her was absolutely filthy.

The tears Charity had held back filled her eyes as the door slammed shut. Amanda came out of the kitchen and gave her a fierce hug. "He's an ass," she whispered. "He was never ever good enough for you."

"You were right," Charity choked. "He was seeing someone else."

Mandy pulled back and looked her sister in the eye. "Don't you dare take him back."

"I won't. I'm done."

The front door of Melk Realty suddenly opened and a gust of wind scattered papers stacked on Charity's desk. She grabbed at them, and placed the stapler on top, before getting up to meet the mailman halfway. "Thank you," she said, taking the bundle of envelopes and magazines.

"My pleasure, Charity. Keep smiling, beautiful."

She gave him a smile and returned to her desk. Her gaze

took in Greg in his office, and part of her hardened, hurt and angry still, and then she told herself he wasn't worth it. She needed to let the anger go. It was time to focus on the things and people that mattered.

Late afternoon, when Rocco's opened at four, she called in an order for a family-size lasagna to go, their famous cheesy garlic bread, plus a green salad. It was expensive, but worth it, she thought when they promised to rush the order and have it ready in forty minutes. She swung by Rocco's at four forty-five, picked up the order and headed out to the Gallaghers' in Paradise Valley.

Her tires crunched snow and ice as she pulled off the highway onto the narrow road lined with big pines that led to the Christmas tree farm.

There were two established tree farms in the area, the Scotts' and the Gallaghers', and her family had always gone to the Gallaghers. She'd grown up thinking it was because her mom had gone to school with Mr. Gallagher, and that might have been part of it, but as Charity and Amanda learned two years ago, they'd gone to the Gallaghers because they always gave her family a tree for free. No one had known but her mom and Mr. and Mrs. Gallagher about the "donation," and when the tree farm passed to their son, Sawyer, he continued the tradition until Mandy and Charity discovered that the Gallaghers had quietly taken care of her family at Christmas for all these years. The sisters had gone to Sawyer and expressed gratitude, insisting that it was time for the tradition to stop because they could afford to buy their parents a tree.

It had been an awkward conversation with Sawyer, not because he had said or done anything uncomfortable, but rather it was uncomfortable knowing while some had scorned the Wrights for their poverty, there were others like the Gallaghers who simply, quietly, lent a helping hand.

Pulling into the gravel parking lot now lit by tall overhead lights, she spotted cars and people, and then finally Quinn, leaning over a vehicle, tying a rather large tree onto the roof of a small car.

She sat in the warmth of her car, just watching, thinking he looked even more gorgeous than she remembered.

She knew it was cold out, but he was working without a coat, wearing a navy patterned wool sweater over some kind of thermal shirt, with the sleeves pushed up to his elbows.

He had fantastic forearms. And hands. She remembered his hands from ice-skating with him in Wyoming, and how he'd tucked the blanket in around her for their sleigh ride.

Turning off the engine, she stepped out of her car and zipped up her parka, trying to get some perspective, which wasn't easy when her heart was racing.

She shouldn't be surprised by the crazy beating of her pulse. From the first time she'd met him at Little Teton Resort, he'd made her heart skip, but it had been almost forty-eight hours since she'd seen him, and the attraction was even stronger than before.

Just looking at him made her feel so many things, and these were totally impractical emotions, but it seemed she had a totally impractical response to him. Charity might not want to feel this pull, but the chemistry wasn't going away.

Charity didn't know if Quinn felt her watching him, or one of the guys said something to him, because he suddenly turned around and looked straight at her, and the corner of his mouth lifted in a slow, sexy smile. She didn't think he was trying to give her a sexy smile. He just *was* sexy.

Why, oh why hadn't she realized he was Quinn Douglas in Wyoming?

It would have made it all so much easier. She would have steered clear of him, and she most definitely wouldn't have opened up so much, sharing those private little tidbits about her life, including highlights from some of her worst dates to the revelation she'd decided two years ago not to have sex again until she married, and men struggled with that. She'd told him that her last boyfriend had used that as an excuse to date someone else, and it had been his defense, too, when people discovered he was two-timing Charity.

No, the late-night sharing by the lodge fire hadn't been a good idea, as the late-night sharing had probably been a case of oversharing, and she wished she could take all of those words back.

Across the lot, Quinn shook hands with the driver of the car, and then started walking toward her. "This is a surprise," he said, closing the distance between them, before wrapping his arms around her and giving her a hug.

He looked big from far away, but close, he felt strong, warm, and hard. He smelled amazing, too—pine, fresh air, and a whiff of spiced shaving cream or aftershave.

He smelled like a man. He smelled like Montana. He smelled like everything she loved. Except she couldn't love this one. He was off-limits, out of bounds, not an option.

"How's it going here?" she asked, slipping from his arms, jamming her hands into her quilted coat pockets. To meet his gaze, she had to tip her head back. His cheeks had a dusky, ruddy glow. The red made his eyes brighter. His teeth shone whiter. He was simply too much of everything.

"It's going well," he answered. "I think I'm starting to get the hang of things. The first day was overwhelming, this morning felt a little less confusing, and now that Sawyer is back, I know we're going to be fine."

"Where is he?"

"He and Jenna are in the house. He wanted to be out here, but Jenna is on bedrest and Sawyer needs to be off his leg, so we've sent them in and made it clear they have to stay there for the night."

"I've brought them dinner," she said. "I'll just carry it in and see if I can help them at all before I go."

"Let me help you. We've salted the parking lot but it's still slippery."

She was glad for his help, and the chance to talk to him a bit more. "Where is your coat? Aren't you freezing?" she asked as they returned to her car.

"It's drying by the fire. I got a massive snowball down the back of my neck and it soaked through on the inside but I'm sure it's dry by now. I should put it on. It's cold."

"Who would do that to you?"

"TJ Sheenan, my nephew, of course."

Charity laughed. "I love that kid. He's all Trey, isn't he?"

"TJ's smart, and I don't know if you know this, but he's got an arm. You should have seen that snowball. He pegged me from twenty yards away."

They carried dinner up to the Gallaghers' log cabin house. Quinn knocked on the door before opening it. "It's Quinn and Charity," he called. "Charity has brought you dinner."

"Come in," Jenna called back. "I'm on the couch. Sawyer is, too. I'm afraid if I get up, I might bump him."

"Stay put," Charity said as they entered the house. "I'll dish you up each a big plate, how's that?"

"What do you have?" Sawyer asked, pushing himself up a bit.

"Rocco's lasagna and some of their garlic bread."

"The cheesy kind?" Jenna asked hopefully.

"The only kind I like," Charity answered. "What do you two want to drink? Milk, water, something else?"

"We both already have water," Jenna answered. "So just food would be fantastic." She nodded at the large take-out container. "And please make up a plate for Quinn. He needs to eat. He worked through lunch without a break."

"It was busy today," Quinn said, opening kitchen cabinet doors looking for plates. He found them and pulled out four. "I'm not eating without you," he said quietly to Charity, "so dish up four servings."

"I can't do that," Charity protested. "I brought this food for Jenna and Sawyer. She can't cook right now."

"Open the refrigerator," he said.

She did. The entire fridge was filled with trays and casserole dishes covered in aluminum foil. "Food has been arriving all day," he added. "There must be at least four lasagnas in there."

"Oh no!" Charity peeled back a couple foil coverings. A crushed chip tuna casserole. Beef stew something. Chicken pot pie. Spaghetti and meatballs. She carefully recovered all the dishes and closed the refrigerator door. "There are no lasagnas," she said.

"The point is, there's a lot of food. Jenna and Sawyer would want you to eat." He gave her a crooked smile. "And maybe it's selfish, but I could use your company."

Her own lips curved in a responding smile. "I suppose I can spare you a half hour. I wish I could give you more, but I'm really popular, wildly in demand."

He laughed his deep, rumbly sexy laugh. The one that made her heart skip a beat and Charity wanted to be in his arms again. "I'll dish them up in here, and then bring plates out to the fire pit. But you better go put your jacket on. No jacket, no dinner."

Charity tossed the salad with Rocco's house dressing, dished huge squares of still-steaming lasagna, and added slices of cheesy garlic bread to Jenna and Sawyer's plates before carrying them into the family room and getting them settled to eat.

"I feel guilty being fussed over," Jenna confessed.

"Don't," Charity answered. "Just rest. I'm going to go eat with Quinn outside but I'll return to check on you and see if you need anything else. If not, I'll do the dishes and sneak out of here."

Sitting on fallen logs by the fire, Charity watched Quinn eat. He ate with fierce concentration at first. Jenna was right. He was hungry. Charity picked at her lasagna and devoured one of the garlic bread slices on her plate feeling ridiculously happy.

"You know," she said after a moment, "I still think this is crazy. You, me, Little Teton, and now here. This is the last thing I expected. It's just too coincidental that we're both from the same town."

"I agree." He looked up at her. "I think there was some divine intervention somewhere. I think we were supposed to meet."

"Ha!"

"You don't think so?" he replied, an eyebrow lifting.

Charity felt a little shiver race through her and she glanced at Quinn from beneath her lashes. "You really think we were supposed to meet?"

"I do."

"Why?"

"Maybe God knew we needed each other."

She swallowed hard, hating the aching lump in her throat, the lump matching the weight in her chest. "Why didn't I recognize you, Quinn? Everyone in town recognizes you."

"You don't like sports. You don't follow sports."

"You must have cringed when I said that in Wyoming."

"I loved it. It was rather... freeing. It's nice to be liked for who you are and not what you do."

She thought about this for a moment. "Do you get a lot of that?"

"There are those who want the lifestyle of being a ball player's girlfriend or wife."

"Is there a lifestyle?"

"Maybe culture is the better word. There is some prestige to it, and there's money. Successful, professional athletes can do very well financially."

"I don't really know anything about that, but honestly, I don't care either."

"I know." He smiled, blue eyes glinting. "And why are you getting mad?"

"I'm not mad. I'm more annoyed with myself than anything. I should have recognized you. It's just... embarrassing. Tricia knew who you were the moment you walked into the travel agency. Sam knew—"

"Sam and I used to get into fist fights. He should know."

She laughed. "Did you really?"

"He was such a pompous little—" Quinn broke off, lifted a hand. "He's grown up. He's changed. I shouldn't have said anything."

"Why would you fight?"

"His family was rich. Mine wasn't."

"Oh."

He scooped up sauce with his crust of bread. "I told you we had more in common than just Marietta."

"True." She shot him a teasing side glance. "We have Sam."

Quinn laughed, the deep husky laugh she adored. "You make me laugh," he said.

"No, you make me laugh, although to be fair, I wasn't laughing in Little Teton when you nearly got us kicked out of the pool."

"You were laughing and we didn't get kicked out."

"We almost did, and I think we would have if I didn't apologize for you."

"I was simply trying to help. You said it wasn't a very hot hot tub. I was just trying to please you by turning up the heat."

"Even though the sign said don't touch the controls?"

Quinn shrugged. "I sometimes take issue with rules, especially if the rules don't make sense."

"Whereas I tend to be a rule follower. I don't like getting in trouble."

"You were so apologetic, when Phil should have apologized to you for being so ridiculously uptight."

"It was his job."

"Now he's the one who needs a sense of humor."

"I won't argue with you on that."

"Incidentally, I spoke to Peter about the not hot enough hot tub, and as it turns out, the heater *was* broken, so it all ended up well."

"Did you say anything to him about Phil?"

"I did."

She shot him a worried glance. "What did you say?"

"That Phil was a very loyal employee, and that was a positive, but he could maybe use a refresher course on customer relations and how to make customers feel valued and wanted."

"How did Peter respond?"

"He agreed that it was probably a good idea to give all employees a crash course in customer service."

She was silent a moment. "I hope the Paces can make it work. It's a really nice place. I thought it was the perfect little ski town."

"I agree."

"Do you… would you… ever consider helping him out?"

"What do you mean?"

She set her plate down and folded her hands in her lap. "You said Peter was a friend."

"Yes."

"Would you help him... financially... if he needed it? Or is that just too much money for you to lend him?"

Quinn reached out to push strands of hair back from her face. "I won't let him lose everything, if that's what you're worried about."

"It can take businesses a while to make a profit. Five years."

"I won't loan more than I can afford to lose," he answered.

"I don't want you to lose anything. I'd structure the loan so you could be a business partner, that way he could benefit from your success and experience."

His lips curved. Creases fanned from his eyes. "Maybe you're the one who should be my business partner. You have a clever head on your shoulders."

"I like business," she said shyly, not certain how he'd react to that. "I haven't ever taken business classes, but I think figuring out how to make a business succeed is interesting, and creative."

"So what is keeping you from starting your own business? Is it the startup costs? The need for space? What's holding you back?"

"I don't know," she admitted. "Those are good questions because I have so many sketches and ideas but I'm just kind of…stuck."

"Then maybe you need to figure out why you're stuck, and don't tell me it's because you're queen of bad decisions. The truth is, you're very smart and you have really good ideas. Maybe it's time you start trusting yourself more." He glanced at his watch and then leaned toward her, and kissed her forehead. "I better get back to work."

Charity watched him walk away, grateful for his faith in her. Quinn had a way of making her feel like she could do anything. Maybe one day she could.

He was right, too. She did need to get 'unstuck' but how was she to do that? That was the part she didn't yet know.

Carrying the plates back into the kitchen, she discovered Jenna seated at the little table in the kitchen. "What are you doing?" Charity scolded, rinsing the plates and loading the dishwasher. "You're supposed to be resting."

"I'm going to bed right after you leave, but I wanted to talk to you about something, and I didn't want Sawyer to hear."

Charity finished with the dishes and joined Jenna at the table. "Is everything okay?"

"I think so, but I'm worried, and I hate to dump this on you, but since you're on the tree auction committee I thought you could give me advice."

"I'll try."

Jenna toyed with the salt shaker on the table. "We'd hoped that by sponsoring this year's tree auction, Gallagher

Tree Farms would get some good exposure, but now with everything that's happened to Sawyer, we're in over our heads and I don't know how to fulfill what we've promised to do. I feel terrible about it."

"What part is worrying you? The financial side?"

"No. Cutting the check was the easy part, and the money went out of our account months ago. It's the rest of it... the table we were supposed to host as the gold sponsor and the big tree we promised to decorate and donate. Last February when they asked us to be the gold sponsor, we didn't know I would be pregnant, and we certainly didn't anticipate Sawyer being hurt. Again." She shook her head. "Sawyer is trying to act like it's not bothering him, but he's upset. He feels like he's let everyone down."

"He hasn't let anyone down. You guys cut that big check months ago and you've been great about getting the word out with flyers next to your cash register. We've nearly sold the event out. We just had a meeting yesterday and we're in really good shape."

"But we can't go now, and we're supposed to host our table and do the tree, impossible when I'm stuck on bedrest."

"That's not a problem. I've got you covered. Hand me your to-do list, big and small, and whatever still needs to be done, I'll do."

"You'll host our table?"

"If that's what you and Sawyer want."

"What about our tree? We haven't even started that because Sawyer and I couldn't agree on a theme." She wrinkled her nose. "Maybe if you have enough trees already for the auction, the committee would be okay scrapping ours?"

Charity glanced out the kitchen window, her gaze taking in the brightly lit barn and the crackling fire and the tall, freshly cut trees in their stands. "No," she said softly. She looked at Jenna. "There's no way we can scrap yours. You're the gold sponsor. We have to have a Gallagher tree represented. The whole point of you underwriting the auction was to get your name front and center."

"I don't have it in me to make it happen."

"You don't have to. I'll do it for you."

A guilty expression crossed Jenna's face. "Before you get too excited, there's something you should know. Sawyer has asked Quinn to help, too, in the event you offered—because he said you would offer—but Sawyer didn't think it was fair for you to get stuck with all the work." Jenna hesitated, and then added in a rush, "And Quinn said yes."

"I have no problem with Quinn," Charity answered, glancing out the window again and searching for him among the trees and customers. He was placing a tree in the baler, getting it wrapped for transport home and just watching him made her heart beat a little faster. She kept telling herself she just wanted to be friends, but her feelings for him were far from platonic. "I'll talk to him on my way out."

Quinn broke away from the customers when he spotted her heading for her car. "Hope you weren't leaving without saying goodbye," he said.

"You looked busy," she answered.

"Never too busy to say goodbye to a friend."

A *friend*. Suddenly Charity found the word *friend* really irritating. She crossed her arms over her chest, mood sour and she didn't even know why. "Jenna wanted me to talk to you about decorating a tree for the tree auction, although it sounds as if you and Sawyer already have it handled."

"We don't have it handled. In fact, I only agreed to do it if you would partner with me. I've never done anything like this but you're artistic and creative and I thought you'd have great ideas."

Quinn's words somewhat mollified her. "Do you have suggestions for a theme?"

"Just one. You probably have a better one. Sawyer has some sports memorabilia from his dad and he thought he could donate it to decorate the tree, giving the tree a sports theme." Quinn's forehead wrinkled. "Specifically baseball."

"Baseball," Charity repeated slowly.

Quinn looked almost embarrassed. "Sawyer has some relatively valuable cards and a couple signed balls and he thought people around here would like them, and that by donating them, the tree would raise more money."

Charity couldn't figure out why Quinn seemed almost shy and then she got it. "Are they your baseball cards?"

He nodded. "It was Sawyer's dad's collection, and Sawyer has been storing it in the attic but I think they want to clear out the attic and I could add to it. I can reach out to the Mariner's front office and ask for some things from the store and get them overnighted. Alice has some of my things, too, in her closet, and she could get them in the mail. But only if you think it's a good idea—"

"I do," she interrupted. "I think this it's pretty perfect, because the best trees are personal. And what's more personal than Quinn Douglas, Marietta's Mr. Baseball, donating a baseball tree?"

He grimaced. "Please don't call me Mr. Baseball. It reminds me too much of how Leo Sterling, Alice's dad, would introduce me to people. It always made my skin crawl. That's not who I am. Here, I'm just Quinn Douglas."

Something in his expression checked her flippant response. He was serious. "I think we have a theme," she said.

"I don't know how to pull it together, though."

"Leave that to me. I've got some ideas. How about I bring us some dinner tomorrow night and show you what I'm thinking?"

"I like the sound of that."

CHAPTER SEVEN

I T HAD ONLY been one day since Sawyer returned from the hospital but he insisted on taking up watch outside by the fire pit where he could monitor the trees and the flow in and out of the barn. Jenna wasn't happy with Sawyer outside, and chose to stay close to his side in a folding chair. Neither of them were smiling, though. Quinn could see the stress in Jenna's face. Something was up but they weren't talking, not to him, or each other.

At noon, when Jenna went into the house for a thicker coat, Quinn headed over to Sawyer. "She's not feeling well, is she?" Quinn asked.

Sawyer's jaw tightened. He glanced toward the house where Jenna had gone. "She needs to be inside, feet up. But she's stubborn and refuses to leave me out here."

"Then why are you out here?"

"You know why."

"Sawyer, look at this place. We have so much help. It seems as if everyone has signed up for a shift—including Carson Scott from Scott Family Christmas Tree Farm. They all want to pitch in and help. Accept the help. Let us make it easier for you two, because as excited as we are about the baby coming, the baby needs to stay put."

Sawyer rubbed the dark bristles on his jaw. "It's not that I don't want the help, but I'm worried about having a lot of strangers on the property. I know they mean well, but the work can be dangerous, look at me. I've been hurt doing this twice now. I'm not comfortable with just anyone baling the trees, or using the chainsaw—"

"I'm going to be here every day, and Rory has signed up to help me, too. We can do this. We won't let you down. And should I have questions, I know where to find you. I'm not afraid to ask for advice or input."

"I can't ask you to be here every day for the next three weeks."

"Maybe you can't, but I'm offering my help. I'm telling you I *want* to do this. And I'm going to show up. Every morning you can look out your window and see my truck pulling in at seven a.m., and I'll stay until you close. And if you need me to stay later because you're extra busy one night, I'm your man. I like a good long game." Quinn cracked a small smile. "Come on. Put me in, coach."

"I owe you."

"No, you don't. I owe you. Just as I owe everyone here in Marietta for taking such good care of us after our folks died. Marietta has always been here for us, and it's my turn to give back."

Silence followed. Sawyer took his time answering. "I

don't think people are looking for payback, Quinn. That's not how we are here in this part of Montana."

"Maybe that's why I really want to do this. Maybe it's why I *need* to do this. It gives me a chance to come home and belong. I haven't felt like I belonged here since I headed off to play ball."

"Is that why you never visit?"

Quinn shrugged. "That big house of mine doesn't quite feel like mine yet."

"It will if you spend enough time here."

Quinn smiled ruefully. "I think that's the plan." He extended a hand to Sawyer. "Now let's get you in the house so Jenna doesn't have to come back out."

Sawyer put his gloved hand into Quinn's and allowed him to help pull him to his feet. "Well in that case, I accept," he said, adjusting the crutches beneath his arms. "Because, apparently, I'm actually doing *you* a favor." He cracked a smile, and then his expression turned thoughtful. "Did Carson Scott really offer to come over and help out here?"

"He did."

"Even though this is his busiest time, too."

"But you'd do the same for him, if the situation was reversed, wouldn't you?"

Sawyer nodded. "Yes. I would."

THE DAY SEEMED to creep by for Charity. She was counting

down the hours until she could head to the tree farm to see Quinn but finally it was almost time for her to leave and she was determined to get out of the office on time.

Greg emerged from his office as she turned off her computer and cleaned off her desk for the night. "Have time for a drink?" he asked.

"I can't. I have plans," she answered, aware that she was already late getting out to the Gallaghers.

"I'm sure you can spare me thirty minutes."

She grabbed her coat and purse and headed out the door. "I really have to go," she said, even as Greg followed her out the door where he grabbed her elbow to stop her.

"Meghan didn't mean anything. We were friends—"

"I don't care, Greg. I really don't."

"Just give me a half hour," he said persuasively, still holding onto her sleeve. "Better yet, let me take you to dinner. I want to fix this. I feel so bad about what happened." He gave her his winning smile; the one she used to think was boyish and charming but now made her stomach knot.

She yanked herself free and took a step away. "We work together, but that's it. We're not friends. We will never be friends. Good night."

"You're making me sound like a bad person. I'm not a bad person."

It was dark out and cold and this part of Main Street was pretty much deserted. Two blocks south Grey's Saloon gleamed with light, but Melk Realty was on a quieter end of the street and Charity wasn't comfortable anymore. "Fine. You're not a bad person. Can I please just go now?"

"You don't realize what a small town this is. People are upset with me, Charity. They're taking their business to other real estate agents. It's not fair to me. We weren't engaged. We weren't married. People need to stop taking sides."

"I agree. It's no one's business but yours and mine."

"Thank you. Now help me fix this."

"Fix it how?" she asked, wrapping her soft knit scarf around her neck.

"I don't know. Spread the word that we're okay. Have a drink with me in public so everyone will know we're on good terms."

She shuddered with distaste. "First of all, I haven't tried to poison anyone. If people are upset, it's because everyone knew about you seeing Meghan and they felt bad for me. I don't like being pitied so this isn't fun for me, either. And in the future, remember that Marietta is a small town and bad news travels fast."

"I need those clients, Charity."

"Then have some integrity," she flashed.

He cursed and reached for her again but suddenly the golden retriever was there, pushing between them, growling at Greg, keeping him back.

"Hey!" Greg exclaimed, swinging his foot at the dog. "Go, get. Scram!"

"Leave him alone," Charity snapped, drawing the dog away from Greg. "What's the matter with you?"

"What's the matter with me? This dog almost attacked—"

"He didn't attack. He just growled at you." She rubbed the retriever's ear, and then the top of his head. The dog's coat was rough. He hadn't been combed in ages.

"He's a menace. I'm going to call the sheriff's office and report him. He's been running around town for the past few days."

"You report him, and I'll report you."

"For what?"

"For threatening my dog."

"He's not your dog."

"Yes, he is."

"Charity, he's not your dog. You don't have a dog. I know. I've been to your house."

"I recently adopted him."

"As in just now?"

"It's none of your business. He's my dog."

"So what's his name?"

"Noel."

"Noel? For a male dog?"

"Yes."

He rolled his eyes, disgusted. "Now who's the liar?"

"I'm not lying. I'm going to keep him until I find his owners."

"He may just be a stray."

"Then maybe he's just found his forever home." She gave Greg a defiant smile, and patted her leg, signaling the dog to follow, and thankfully, Noel did.

RORY COULDN'T GET out to the tree farm for the afternoon as he'd promised, and Trey Sheenan, McKenna's husband, came in his place.

Once upon a time Trey had been a huge problem for Quinn and Rory, but now that Trey and McKenna were finally together, settled and strong, Trey had become someone the entire family relied on. Trey had completely turned his life around, and that transformation inspired Quinn, and reaffirmed his belief in a higher power.

But even with his faith, Quinn struggled with his purpose. People liked to tell him that there was a reason he hadn't died in the tragedy at the ranch, but he hadn't discovered that purpose yet.

As a teenager, Quinn had wrestled with questions and doubts, and sometimes the doubts returned. In those moments he prayed for strength, not wanting to let his parents down, aware that he was their legacy, and that he needed to succeed for them, to prove that they had been good people, loving people, and that their love and life hadn't been in vain.

He told no one this.

He was an athlete, and people wanted him to make great

plays and provide entertainment, but at home, when he was alone, he felt an aching awareness that there should be more.

He was supposed to do more.

But what?

Perhaps the plan had not yet been revealed, and maybe the challenge was to keep believing. His parents had lived in faith. They had reached out to everyone, giving to all. Their generosity had sometimes made it difficult for them to pay their bills, but he would have it no other way.

Friends mattered, family mattered, community mattered. Community helped him heal after he was injured. Everyone in Marietta had wished him well, rallying around the three of them—Rory, Quinn and McKenna—and he'd been so grateful for the support that once he was back at high school, every time there was a local fund-raiser, he took part. Every time there was a car wash or a trash pickup, he volunteered. He did that all the way through high school and college. But after being drafted he didn't come home as much, not intentionally distancing himself from Marietta, but he was focused on his career, thinking that maybe he'd do something in baseball that would matter. But in the end, his athletic accomplishments weren't that significant. He wasn't one of the greats; he'd never join the Hall of Fame.

Quinn felt the clap of a firm hand on his back.

"You all right?" Trey's deep voice asked gruffly.

Quinn grimaced. "Am I exuding bad vibes?"

Trey gave him another firm pat on the back and then

shoved his hands in his coat pockets. "You wouldn't know how to exude bad vibes, and that's saying something because I know what you have been through."

"I don't think of it that way. I'm one of the lucky ones."

"That doesn't mean coming home isn't hard for you. Things have changed since you were the most valuable player at Marietta High."

Quinn's lips twisted. "It's more complicated now, for sure."

"It takes time to make a place home, not easy when your job is on the West Coast." Trey paused. "But it helps when there is something, or someone here, that calls you back."

"You mean family."

"Or a pretty girl."

Quinn shot him a swift glance but said nothing.

Trey grinned, a lazy cocky smile before nodding toward the parking lot where Charity had just pulled in. "And look, here she is."

CHARITY GOT OUT of the car and carefully closed the door, telling Noel she'd be right back. Noel whined softly and she tried to give him a reassuring smile.

He'd behaved beautifully on the drive from town, sitting in the passenger seat beside her, looking out the window as if this was an everyday occurrence, and maybe it was. Maybe his owner used to take him everywhere. Maybe he had a family that was missing him desperately right now. She'd have to call the local shelter and get Noel checked by a local vet to see if he had a chip that might identify him since he wore no collar. But until then, she wasn't about to leave him where Greg could get to him.

Quinn had been talking to Trey Sheenan when Charity pulled up and broke away from Trey when she parked. He was walking her way now and she stood her ground, not sure how he'd react to her having a stray dog in her car, but not about to abandon Noel now that she had him.

Quinn spotted the retriever before Charity could even say anything. "I didn't know you had a dog," he said.

"I don't," she answered, zipping up her coat against the cold.

"Is it your parents'?"

"He's been wandering around downtown Marietta for a few days and I was worried about him. I didn't want anything to happen to him."

"So he's going to live in your car?"

She laughed, because she could see the teasing light in Quinn's lovely blue eyes. "No. In the morning, I'm going to take him in to the vet and see if he has a microchip. Hopefully, I can find the owner, but until I do, I'll take care of him."

"He's friendly?"

"He growled at Greg."

"Good dog."

Charity's lips curved and her heart squeezed, making the air catch in her throat. Something about Quinn made her see possibilities.

She could see herself watching the evening news with him at the end of the day, going to church with him, and lacing up their skates at Miracle Lake on weekends. In January, when the days were long and dark, they could go to a movie and have dinner at the Chinese restaurant afterward. And on the nights when it rained and the wind howled, they'd be safe and warm together.

There was a whole life that could be lived with Quinn. She wanted that life, but was it an impossible dream?

"Want to meet Noel?" she asked.

Quinn choked on a muffled laugh. "Noel?"

"Don't make the same mistake Greg did. It's a great name."

"I just thought the dog didn't have any tags?"

"Noel doesn't, but it's almost Christmas and the name suits him."

Quinn opened the door and crouched down, letting the dog decide if he wanted to go to Quinn.

Noel did.

Noel raced toward him, tongue hanging out, apparently thrilled by this new human. Quinn rubbed Noel's neck, and then gave him a good scratch behind the ear. Noel's tail thumped happily. Quinn crooned something that pleased Noel so much that the dog's tongue swiped the side of

Quinn's face.

"I think Noel likes you," Charity said, inordinately pleased by how quickly the two were bonding. "I told Greg he's a good dog. There's no way I'm going to let animal control take him."

"What if you can't find his owners?"

"I'll keep him."

His eyebrow shot up. "Just like that?"

"Well, not just like that. I'll have to find a new place to live. Mom is allergic to dogs, but it's time I had my own place, and this way I won't be alone. I'll have Noel."

"Whoa. Slow down. Noel may have owners desperate to get him back."

"I think that's probably true, and I'm going to work on it tomorrow. It's Saturday. I have the whole day off. But if he doesn't have a home I want him. He was there for me earlier today, and I want to be there for him."

Quinn's expression changed. "What happened earlier?"

"Greg was getting a little handsy and Noel appeared out of nowhere and stepped between us and growled at Greg." She glanced at the handsome dog that seemed to be listening intently, and she flashed Noel a grateful smile. "What a good boy he is."

QUINN KEPT HIS voice calm even as he saw red. "What do you mean by handsy?" he asked. "What exactly did Greg do?"

"He was just grabbing at me and Noel didn't like it."

"Grabbing at you?"

"He likes to try to intimidate me, but I'm not intimidated. He forgets that I was raised on Chance Avenue. Growing up, it was the rough part of town."

"How long has this been going on? And why?"

"He's upset that he's lost business because of me."

"That's his fault," Quinn said tersely. "Not yours."

"I know."

"He's not a victim and he has no business turning this onto you. I—" Quinn broke off, unwilling to finish the sentence. But that didn't mean he was going to let this slide. He took a slow breath, trying to calm down. He glanced from Charity to the big dog. "So if you can't take Noel home, where is he staying tonight?"

She gave him a hopeful look. "With you?"

He pictured his big, empty house.

She lifted her hands, pressing them together in a prayerful pose. "Please?"

Looking down into her beautiful face, he was a goner. This was his woman. He couldn't resist her. He couldn't disappoint her. Maybe he wasn't on earth for ball. Maybe he was still here for her. "Noel can stay with me tonight," he said.

She flung her arms around him. "Thank you! Thank you, thank you, thank you."

He held her close for a moment before letting her go. "My pleasure."

Cars had been pulling in while they talked and the Christmas tree lot was filling quickly with people.

"I better get back to work," he said. "Are we still eating dinner later?"

Her mouth opened, and then closed. "Oh no, I totally forgot. Things were weird at work and then I was so worried about Noel—"

"It's fine."

"I'll go get something."

"Don't. Please. Jenna has been keeping a tuna casserole in the oven warm for me. I'll just have some of that later."

"I'm really sorry."

"I don't care." He pulled her back toward him and pressed a kiss to her forehead. "I'm just glad you're here." He meant it, too. He liked having her near. Everything was better when she was close by. He let her go but she didn't step away. He liked that, too.

"What if I go up to the house and see if Jenna and Sawyer mind if Noel hangs out with me while you work?" she said.

"Good idea," he said. "And make sure you have some of that tuna casserole, too."

CHARITY POPPED HER head into the Gallaghers' house. Jenna

and Sawyer were on the couch, side by side, watching the evening news. Sawyer's arm was around Jenna's shoulder, and his injured leg was up on the ottoman, his crutches nearby. Jenna's head was on her husband's shoulder and her hand rested on her round belly. They looked incredibly cozy and happy, just the way a young family should. This was what she wanted one day. A friend, a partner, unconditional love.

"Hate to intrude," she said, stepping into the family room, "but wanted to check in on you guys. Everything okay?"

Sawyer gave her a thumbs-up sign.

"Doing well," Jenna said, giving her belly a light rub. "Thankfully this one has settled back down."

"Very good news," Charity said.

Sawyer gestured to the kitchen. "Quinn's dinner is in the oven. Is he coming in to eat, or are you taking him a plate?"

"I'll take him a plate as soon as he has a break," Charity answered. "But I do have a question for you. Not sure how you feel about dogs, but I have a golden retriever in my car and I'd love to let him out to stretch his legs. Would you have a problem with that?"

"When did you get a dog?" Jenna asked.

"He's lost, I think. I'm going to take him to Dr. Sullivan's in the morning to see if he's been microchipped, and Quinn said he'd keep Noel for the night—"

"Noel?" Sawyer interrupted.

Charity made a face. "Why do guys not like that name? Never mind. Don't answer. Let me go get him."

Noel was delighted to be out of the car and walked next to Charity as they crossed the parking lot and headed for the house. Inside, he was a perfect gentleman. He sat when commanded and then put his paw in Sawyer's hand when Sawyer said shake.

"He's been well trained," Sawyer said, impressed.

"And well loved," Jenna added. "Look how sweet he is."

Sawyer gave the dog a good pat, examining Noel's coat, and then pressing against his side. "He's pretty thin. You can feel each rib. I have a feeling he's been on his own for some time."

Charity nodded. "He's been wandering around downtown for the past few days, but where did he come from? Whose dog is he?"

"I don't know, but we need to feed him," Jenna said. "We still have the rest of that huge meatloaf from lunch. Mix it with some of the leftover rice in there. I bet he'd love it."

"Does the meatloaf have onions?"

"Not this recipe."

"Good. Let's see if he likes it."

Noel *loved* his dinner. He devoured everything and then drank water from the bowl provided and, stomach full, followed Charity back outside to the fire pit in front of the barn and flopped down at her feet. They sat for a half hour watching Quinn work.

Charity didn't know what Noel was thinking, but she was thinking she was really going to miss Quinn when he returned to Seattle. And he would return. If not before Christmas, then after. He had to get back to his routine, and the gym, and the trainer he used to keep him in shape for the upcoming season.

She tried to imagine herself in Seattle. It was a huge leap, but if she and Quinn did date, and if it did work, would he want a long distance relationship?

Would she?

And if the dating turned serious, what then?

Quinn took a photo with a man and his son and she smiled to herself, thinking he was such a lovely man. Then he glanced at her and winked and her heart turned over.

It was really cold tonight and yet he made her feel impossibly warm and tender.

Maybe it was time to admit she had feelings for him, and they weren't the platonic kind. She didn't view him as a buddy or a pal. When she thought of him, she just melted… there was no other way to describe it.

Quinn walked over to her, and Noel lifted his head, tail wagging as Quinn approached. "I get twenty minutes for a dinner break."

"I'll grab the plates of casserole," Charity said, jumping to her feet. "You sit down and rest. I'll be right back."

The television was off in the family room and the downstairs was quiet. Sawyer and Jenna must have gone to bed.

Charity tiptoed in to the kitchen and dished up the casserole onto paper plates, turned off the oven, grabbed plastic utensils, and headed back outside.

"I think they've gone to bed," she said, handing Quinn a plate and sitting down next to him.

"Good. They need the rest."

They ate for a few minutes in silence and then Quinn asked, "Any thoughts on that baseball Christmas tree idea?" he asked, blowing on his cocoa to cool it.

She nodded and setting her plate down, pulled out a sheet of paper from her coat pocket. It was a watercolor sketch of a tall tree covered in red, blue, and white ribbon, with baseball card ornaments, topped by a ball and glove.

"That's pretty. Very pretty. I like it," Quinn said, "but how are you going to hang the cards? You're not putting a hole in them, are you?"

"No, absolutely not. Here, let me show you these pictures I found on Pinterest." She pulled out her phone from the other pocket and opened it to her photos. "We'd put all the baseball cards in little plastic sleeves like these and attach them to the tree with a narrow red and white ribbon. See how it looks like the thread on a baseball? I have to order the ribbon but that's not a problem. I can have it here by the end of the week, and the sleeves will make sure the signed cards won't be hurt so they won't affect the value."

"Perfect."

She went to another photo of different colored glass

balls. "I'm going to shop for some red and blue balls, and see if I can find any ornaments that are shaped like stars. I think they'll add a fun touch, because as we all know, you did play in the all-star game for years."

She turned to yet another photo. "I'm not sure what Mr. Gallagher collected, or what you can get from the Seattle Mariner store, but if we can get a bunch of pennants, either Seattle ones, or I can even order some from the different cities you played ball in, and I will stitch them together and create a fun tree skirt."

"Now that's really cool. I like that."

"If you have any bobble heads, I can make ornaments out of those. I'll be sure not to damage them, because serious collectors will want them in excellent condition. Signed balls can go in acrylic boxes and we'd hang them from the bigger branches. And lastly, if you have an old glove you can donate, and maybe a signed ball, we will put them on the top of the tree like this, instead of the traditional angel or star."

He nodded approvingly. "I like all of it. I do."

"Now we just need to see what Mr. Gallagher has and then supplement with whatever you can get sent here."

"I'll call the Mariners' front office tomorrow and also ask Alice to mail the box she's been keeping for me."

"Tomorrow, after I take Noel to the vet, I'll order the ribbon, plastic sleeves, and acrylic boxes. If I do rush shipping they should be here almost right away."

"Let me know how much it all costs and I'll reimburse

you."

"That's not necessary."

"I want to."

"I don't doubt that but, Quinn, I don't want your money. Let me do my part, okay?"

He gestured to the sketch. "It looks you're going to be doing more than your fair share."

"It'll be a fun project and, honestly, it won't take me that long. Oh, and there's one more idea. It's something I can do right away because I can get everything I need from the Mercantile." She picked up her phone again and zoomed in on the photo of a tree covered in glowing lights. "See these baseball lights? They're actually miniature white lights tucked inside ping-pong balls that have been painted to look like the threads on a baseball."

"It's certainly cool, but Charity, that looks like way too much work."

"I don't have to cover every single little light with a ball. I can do it every third or fourth light, and honestly, it shouldn't take that much time. One evening."

"But aren't you also making your sister a dress for the gala?"

"Yes. But that's not a problem. I like to be busy. If I'm home, I have to keep my hands busy."

His lashes dropped and his gaze rested on her face. "What about you? What are you wearing to the gala?"

There was something intimate in his inspection and she

felt her cheeks warm. "I don't know yet. I'll figure it out."

"I hope it's special. You deserve to feel special."

"Because we're hosting the Gallagher's table?"

"Because you deserve a dress that is as beautiful as you."

The air bottled in her lungs. For a moment she couldn't breathe. She ducked her head, suddenly shy. "That's very nice of you."

"Charity," he said.

She lifted her head to look at him. "Yes?"

"Will you go to the Mistletoe and Montana auction with me?"

Her mouth opened, closed. "We're already cohosting."

"Right. I know. But I'd like you to go with me. To be my date." He lifted a brow. "What do you think?"

She hesitated, and then nodded. "Yes." She nodded again, unable to hide her smile. "I can't wait."

CHAPTER EIGHT

CHARITY LEFT RIGHT after dinner. By eight thirty, the parking lot was empty. At nine, Quinn turned off all the lights and music, locked up the barn, put out the fire, and left the barn key underneath the Gallaghers' back mat.

He drove back to his place with Noel on the seat beside him, making a call to Sam Melk as he drove. His call went to voice mail but he left a short message for Sam to call him back ASAP, confident Sam would.

He then thought of Charity and how cute she'd looked when she agreed to be his date for the gala. Her shy smile made him feel like he'd just asked her to the senior prom. She made him feel so good. Spending time with her was easy. Even in Wyoming, when they knew virtually nothing about each other, Quinn had been so comfortable, and so at ease in his own skin. From the first time they talked, he'd felt like himself... just better.

For the most part, he was a happy person, because happiness was a choice. Life was short—he'd learned that one young—and he wasn't going to waste a single day on anger, bitterness, or resentment. No, he'd focus on the good things, and the good people, and just like that, he heard Charity's voice in his head. *If I'm home, I have to keep my hands busy.*

Those words she'd spoken by the fire had made his chest tighten. His mom used to say the same thing. She would knit at night as they gathered in the family room, the news on for his dad, or a family-friendly show for the kids, and when she finished the dishes, and emerged from the kitchen, she'd sit in the corner of the sofa closest to his father's chair, and knit away, needles clicking, yarn unraveling.

The *click-click* sound had always reassured him. It meant she was there with them. It meant she was finally off her feet and able to relax. His mom had worked harder than anyone he knew. She'd been a fantastic mother, and he'd never said it enough. But he was also sure that she knew, and that she understood just how deeply she was loved.

Moms were important. Women were important. No man should ever treat a woman badly, for any reason. In Quinn's mind, intimidating women was nothing short of a crime.

Quinn was almost home when his phone rang. His Bluetooth announced Sam Melk. Good. Just the man he wanted to talk to. "Sam," he said, as he turned up his long dark drive. "Thanks for calling me back. I know it's getting late."

"Always available for my friends and clients. My wife complains, but I work twenty-four seven," Sam's voice was cheerful and hearty. "I'm hoping you're interested in selling your place, not that I want to lose you here but it's something special—"

"No." Quinn parked in front of his sprawling six-thousand-foot house and turned his engine off. The truck lights went out, too. It was pitch dark and Noel lifted his head, and glanced uneasily out the window. "Let's just cut to the chase. Do you really not know that Greg is giving Charity a hard time? Does this strike a chord, or is this coming out of left field?"

"Probably no pun intended, huh?" Sam joked, before sighing. "Okay, I'll be serious. I'm aware that there is considerable tension in the office. It's actually pretty miserable for everyone right now."

"This is your business and these are your employees, but I'm concerned about what's going on, and have an issue with how Greg is treating Charity."

"Has something specific happened?"

"Greg is putting his hands on her, and it needs to stop."

"I agree."

"I don't want to have to step in, but if I need to, I'll show him some good old-fashioned Montana diplomacy."

"I remember your Montana diplomacy. I had bruises for a week."

Noel shifted and rested his head on Quinn's knee. Quinn gave the dog's ear a little tug. "I'm sure you know how to handle your own employees, so I can leave this to you?"

"Yes."

"Great. Thanks for your time, Sam. Good talk."

"Good night."

"Night." Quinn hung up and stepped out of the truck. He called Noel's name, patted his leg, and the retriever jumped out, following Quinn up the walkway.

Quinn made a mental note to leave his porch light on when he left the house in the morning for the Gallaghers. It grew dark early in Seattle this time of year, but here in Paradise Valley it was even darker without streetlights and big buildings to brighten the night sky. As he fumbled with his key in the front door's dead bolt, his shoulder brushed something soft and cushy. He lifted a hand and touched it. Round. Some kind of greenery. And fabric.

Swinging the front door open, Quinn turned on the porch light and studied the oversized wreath with vintage silver, red and green glass balls. Someone had hung a wreath on his door.

Someone had given him a Christmas present. He suspected he knew who that someone was, too, as his sister-in-law Sadie loved everything vintage, and she was probably the craftiest person he'd ever met.

He was touched, really touched, and while it hadn't crossed his mind to get anything festive for the house, it clearly needed a little bit of holiday charm. Impulsively he phoned Sadie to thank her for the present, but when she answered, she denied knowing anything about a wreath. "It sounds pretty, though," she said. "Take a picture and send it to me."

He did, and she texted back that it was even more beautiful than he'd described, and suggested that maybe he should check with Charity or McKenna.

He texted both, neither knew anything about it. Or so they claimed. Quinn didn't know what to make of that.

Closing the front door, he gave Noel a brief tour of the downstairs. "Kitchen," he said, turning on the light. "Dining room. Great room. Guest bath. Smaller family room. Downstairs guest bedroom down the hall." The dog trailed Quinn obediently, going from room to room with him before they ended back up in the kitchen.

"I'm still hungry," Quinn confessed.

Noel cocked his head.

"You look hungry, too," Quinn added.

Noel's head cocked the other way.

"You're a good boy." Quinn gave the dog's head another pat. "I kind of like you. And it's nice to have someone here to talk to."

Quinn opened the refrigerator. It was virtually empty. On one shelf was a white Styrofoam take-out container from Rocco's, and a half-eaten roast beef sandwich wrapped in paper was on another shelf, the sandwich left over from the day he drove from Jackson Hole. It might be time to buy some groceries and settle in since he was staying through Christmas.

Quinn went into the pantry, huge bottles of water lined

the floor. Cleaning supplies. Not much else.

"We need to shop," he told Noel. "Tomorrow we'll get you some food. In the meantime, tonight we have Rocco's leftover gnocchi and that roast beef. How about I do the gnocchi and you do the beef?"

Noel's tail thumped once.

"Good answer," Quinn replied. While the gnocchi warmed in the microwave, he filled a medium-size bowl with water for Noel and put it on the kitchen floor in the corner. The microwave dinged and he heated the meat from the sandwich for a few seconds so it wouldn't be so cold. It didn't take long for them to eat. There wasn't much, and Quinn was ready to call it a night.

He took Noel out the back door, walked him to the snow-covered grass. "Go pee," he said.

Noel walked around a moment, sniffing here and there before doing what he was told.

"Good boy," Quinn praised him. "Now let's see if we can get you to sleep."

Upstairs in the huge master bedroom, Quinn made up a bed for Noel on the ground next to his bed. He took two quilts folded them and then added a fleece blanket on top. "Spot," Quinn said, pointing to the blankets.

Noel hesitated and then went to the bed and circled once, and then again, before lying down.

"Good boy, good Noel," Quinn praised him, climbing into his bed. Quinn turned out the light, punched the pillow a couple of times, and almost immediately fell asleep.

When he woke up in the morning, Noel was on the bed, sleeping next to him.

Quinn yawned and grinned. It seemed like Noel had made himself at home.

CHARITY WOKE UP to a text from Quinn telling her that Rory was going to open the tree farm for him so he could get to town for some groceries, and since he was heading her way, why didn't he meet her at the vet's office with Noel?

Charity quickly answered that it was a great idea.

Quinn texted that he was leaving his house now, and asked her to send him the name of the veterinarian she used, as well as the address.

After sending him the name and address for Dr. Noah Sullivan's practice in Marietta, she pulled her hair up into a ponytail, covered it with a shower cap and hopped in the shower.

Dressed, she filled a travel mug with hot coffee, said goodbye to her mom who was doing a Sudoku puzzle, then waved to her father who was watching morning news in front of the TV, and then headed out.

It was cold this morning but clear, the sky almost too bright for her eyes. Icicles hung from the eaves of the house and the windows of her car were covered in a thick, hard ice coat.

JANE PORTER

Charity scraped the ice from her windshield as her car warmed up. She was looking forward to seeing Quinn and couldn't wait to hear how Noel had done last night. Hopefully, he hadn't been too much trouble.

She arrived at Dr. Sullivan's and discovered Quinn was already there, his black rental truck parked in front of the entrance.

She peeked inside his truck and saw it was empty and then went on in to the veterinary office. Carols played in the waiting area. A Christmas tree sat in the corner and mistletoe hung from the ceiling.

Opening the door she discovered Quinn at the front desk talking to the white-haired receptionist, who wore reindeer antlers, with Dr. Sullivan there, too, just behind the receptionist, while Noel lay on the ground at Quinn's feet.

"Have I kept you waiting?" Charity asked anxiously.

Quinn shook his head. "No, I only got here a few minutes ago but he does have a microchip, only Dr. Sullivan didn't need to use it. The staff here recognized Rusty right away."

Rusty.

Her heart sank. So he did have an owner. She should be glad for Rusty.

"Will Dr. Sullivan notify the owner that we have Noel—Rusty?" she asked, trying to hide her disappointment.

"That's the good news, bad news part," Quinn said to her. "Rusty was a service dog, and his owner, Mary, lived here in town on Church Street. Mary passed away a couple of years ago and Rusty has taken it very hard. Although Rusty was placed almost right away with a new family, he's proven difficult to rehome. The latest owners, a family that lives north of Livingston, don't want him back. They vowed that if Rusty ran away again, they'd let him go. It's too hard on their son every time Rusty leaves."

"That makes me sad. Poor Rusty," Charity said, stroking the top of the dog's head. "It's been years and yet he's still looking for Mary."

"That's also a long way for him to walk," Quinn added. "He's lucky he hasn't been hurt."

Charity looked at the doctor. "So what happens to Rusty now?"

"You'll need to take him to the animal shelter and they'll see if they can find a new family for him, or…" His voice trailed off.

"I want him," she said decisively. "I want to adopt him. How do I do that?"

"The county would say he still needs to go to the shelter—"

"No." Her voice was firm. "I don't trust those places."

"Crawford County's is better than most," he answered.

"That's not good enough for me or Rusty," she said. "Can't you reach out to the current owner and see if they would allow me to adopt him? Or give me the number and I'll call them? He's a loving dog and I think he just needs a home in Marietta."

"He might still wander," Quinn warned her.

She looked down into Rusty's warm brown eyes. He gazed steadily back at her, his tail thumping. "But he might not," she answered, petting him. "He might be happy with me."

"First, we should get him checked out. Make sure he's healthy." Quinn glanced at Noah. "Can you do a physical? See if there is anything we should be worried about."

Charity heard how Quinn said *we. If there is anything we should be worried about.*

His words warmed her. She liked having him on her team. "That's probably smart," she agreed.

"Can we leave him here now, or do we need to make an appointment?"

"We could take him now. But if you're not planning on boarding him for the night, be back before we close."

"He needs to be fed," Quinn added. "I'll pick up a bag of whatever food you recommend, but he hasn't eaten this morning, and he only had people food last night."

"We'll take care of Rusty," Noah promised. "And we'll make some calls and let you know what his current owners want to do."

Charity gave Rusty a hug and told him she'd be back for him in just a couple of hours. Quinn left his number with the front desk, and asked that he be called as soon as they had any news, one way or the other.

Outside the office, Charity faced Quinn. "Thank you," she said gratefully. "For all your help with Noel."

The corner of his mouth curled. "You're not going to call him Rusty?"

"He answers to Noel."

He laughed. "You're something," he said, drawing her into his arms and holding her there a moment before releasing her. "I better get to the Gallaghers. It's supposed to be very busy today."

She'd liked being in his arms. She'd felt good there. "I'm going to be working on the tree," she said.

"I'll let you know when Rusty can be picked up."

"Can I bring him to you?"

"I think you should."

He reached for his keys but he didn't walk away.

She couldn't make herself leave, either. "Quinn?"

"Yes?" he answered, his gaze locking with hers.

She felt lost in his eyes, and she held her breath as emotions washed over her. She liked him. She liked him so much. Did he have any idea how she truly felt? Finally, she exhaled and then said, "For the record, I like being on your team."

His jaw eased and his smile was crooked. "For the record, I do, too."

Charity thought about Quinn and Noel all day, and she itched to go see Quinn but she would never get Amanda's dress done, or the tree decorations made, if she kept running around instead of staying in one place and working.

She was about to call Dr. Sullivan's office when Quinn phoned her. "I've just heard from Noah. They want to keep Rusty Noel overnight," he said.

"Why?"

"Noah has to file some paperwork with the county, and he needs to have Rusty there when he processes the paperwork requesting adoption. It's a county ordinance."

"Noel is not going to like being there all night."

"I know, and it's frustrating, but it's just for the night. We should be able to pick him up in the morning."

"Okay," she said, reluctantly, trying not to feel discouraged. She was tired and lonely and she really wished she and Quinn could have more together time. She felt like she was only seeing him in little stolen moments now and then. "So how is it going there?"

"Great. Slammed. We've gone through so much stock. It's getting a little thin in the yard. Sawyer said we might need to go to the back lot and get some more trees."

"You sound excited about that."

"It is kind of exciting. I like the work. Speaking of work, I better go. It's hectic here at the moment. I'm sorry."

"No, that's okay. Just take care of yourself."

"You, too." And then he hung up.

CHARITY SPENT SUNDAY morning in Bozeman buying

ornaments and the craft supplies she needed for the Gallaghers' tree. She was just finishing shopping when she got a text from Quinn that she could go pick up Rusty.

She returned to Marietta and collected the retriever who was delighted to see her, and together they headed out to the Gallaghers.

The tree lot was filled with families and Quinn was being pulled in so many directions that he nodded at Charity but couldn't break away to talk. Hoping that things would slow, Charity went into the Gallaghers' cute log cabin house and visited with Jenna while they made a batch of Grandma Gallagher's famous sugar cookies before Charity took another walk around the festive barn, still hoping Quinn could break free, but it didn't happen.

She bundled her arms across her chest and exhaled. She missed Quinn. She missed being alone with Quinn. She missed feeling special and important to him.

And there was nothing inside of her that just wanted to be his friend.

She wanted to be his, and only his, and she wanted him to be hers. It was time he knew that, too. It was time they figured out their relationship and she'd been the one holding back but she was done playing it safe.

Charity checked that Noel was safe with Jenna and Sawyer, before returning to her car and driving home.

Rather than dwell on the fact that Quinn had been too busy to spend time with her, she'd just tackle her very long to-do list, and at the top of her list, was painting tiny red dashes to look like thread on the four-dozen ping-pong balls.

By midafternoon she'd painted all the balls and washed her brushes and was plugging in her glue gun to take on the next task when Quinn called.

"Your sister and her husband have just shown up here," he said, "and they're cutting me loose. Apparently they spoke to Rory and Sawyer and they've all conspired to send me away from here. I have to leave, now, and I've been given strict orders to go do something fun."

"Those are your instructions? To do something fun?"

"Yes. That's why I'm calling you. I need your help. Can you possibly think of something fun we could do together?"

Warmth rushed through her and she found herself smiling. "Well, you could come over here and hot glue ribbons onto plastic sleeves with me."

"Hmm, I wouldn't call that fun."

"We could grocery shop."

"Definitely not fun."

"Wrap gifts?"

"I'm really beginning to think you don't know how to play."

She smiled at his scolding tone. "Or... we could do something boring like ice skate."

"Funny girl. I'm leaving here now to pick you up as Miracle Lake is calling."

She unplugged the glue gun, got to her feet and

stretched. "You don't have to come all the way into town. I can meet you there."

"No, I've missed you. I look forward to catching up."

"What about Rusty Noel?"

"He can stay here. He loves all the activity and attention he gets. I'll get him on my way home."

QUINN PULLED UP to the small blue house on Chance Avenue and called Charity. "I'm out front," he said, when she answered. "Shall I come to the door? I'd like to say hello to your dad. It's been a long time since high school."

"Maybe next time," she said, sounding anxious. "Dad is watching some crime show and Mom is napping and Mom never sleeps so I'd just as soon let her keep sleeping."

"Okay, I'll just wait out here then."

"I won't be long. Sorry to keep you waiting."

He left the truck engine running, and used the time to study her neighborhood. The street didn't look as rough as it had been when he was in school, but Chance Avenue was still shabby. Houses were small. The fences dividing properties were mostly chain link. Dirty snow piled in the driveways and along the curb. The Wrights' house was blue, and the paint was peeling off in places. There were no shutters at the windows. Nothing about the front yard, or steps, inspired confidence. It was winter, and Montana took a beating in winter, but there could have been some charm somewhere.

It couldn't have been easy for Charity and her sisters to go to Marietta High, knowing that just one street over were all the big, handsome turn-of-the-century houses on Bramble, and that her school was filled with students that had so much more.

Charity might not care about material things, but the lack of material things had shaped her.

The front door suddenly opened and Charity came bounding down the steps and over to the truck, skates in her hand.

He climbed out of the truck and went round to open her door. She thanked him before getting in, adding, "It took me a minute to clean up my mess and then find my skates. This is the first time I've skated this year so they were still put away."

Settling into her seat, Charity clutched the battered skates to her chest and gave him a blindingly bright smile. "I'm so excited we're doing this."

Quinn had known he was falling for her for a long time. He'd been drawn to her immediately when they first met, and every moment they spent together—or even apart—only cemented his feelings, but it was the moment she flashed her bright, beautiful smile, and told him how excited she was to skate, he knew he loved her. He hadn't just fallen in love with her, but he loved *her*.

She was undemanding and selfless and cheerful and kind

and it killed him that she asked for so little, when she deserved the sun and the moon and all the stars.

"It's going to be dark soon," he said, once he was back in the driver's seat, "but I heard they've installed lighting now."

She nodded. "They did that a couple years ago. But everything else is pretty much the same."

"I'll need to rent skates," he said.

"The skate shack will be open."

"Let's go then."

IT WASN'T AS crowded at Miracle Lake as Charity had expected. Most of the families with younger kids were gone, leaving the frozen lake to teenagers and adults, which was a good thing as Quinn had decided to challenge Charity to a skate-off, wanting to prove he was the superior skater and then doing everything in his power to keep her from winning their races—even if it meant relying on some underhanded tactics.

Fortunately, even with his tactics she was still beating him half the time. "You are unbelievably competitive," she said, laughing and gulping in air as she slowly glided around the rink, letting her burning muscles cool. "Maybe it's time you accepted that I just might be better than you."

"Not going to happen," he flashed, giving her a lethal smile as he caught her hands and drew her toward him.

"Your baseball contracts don't let you ski," she said, as he skated backward, and her skates moved inside his so they glided effortlessly across the ice. "But skating is fine."

"I'm sure it's probably not encouraged, but I don't remember it being part of paragraph 5b."

"What else can't you do?"

"Sky diving, rock climbing, hang gliding, motorcycle riding, boxing, auto racing, spelunking, snowmobiling, and participating in rodeos."

"So skating is okay?"

"I'd only get in trouble if I got hurt."

"In that case, let's get you skating forward, just to be on the safe side. Life is hard enough without adding in the element of danger."

He changed his hold and did an easy turn so that he now skated next to her. "What's hard about life?"

She flashed to her childhood and her memories of growing up and the daily struggle to just get by, without being hungry or uncomfortable or humiliated for not being groomed enough, or good enough. She'd never forget the day in second grade when someone told her in the morning lineup that she smelled, reeking like pee, and by the time they were allowed in to the classroom, all the kids were whispering that she'd peed her pants, but Charity hadn't.

Her teacher even pulled her aside and sniffed her, and then sniffed her coat and backpack. The backpack was fine, but the coat and the sweater beneath did reek of pee. Charity was mortified. Even more mortified when her mother came to school with clean clothes. Charity begged her mother to let her go home with her but her mother said she had to stay.

It wasn't until it happened again, that she understood her dad was getting so drunk he was mistaking the laundry basket for a urinal.

"Life wasn't easy when I was growing up," she said to Quinn. "It was unpredictable—for years. I craved safety. People I could count on. Situations that were stable. Change represented chaos, and chaos was pain."

They circled the rink again, the blades on their skates scraping the ice. "Was there anything that made you feel safe when you were a little girl?" he asked after a moment.

She didn't even need to think about it. "My sisters. Jenny and Mandy. I wouldn't even be me without them."

"I feel that way about Rory and McKenna," he said.

She gave his hand a little squeeze. "You all went through so much. You lost so much."

"I got off lucky, though, compared to Rory," he answered. "He saw it all. He returned to find the aftermath, and because of that, he has horrific images burned in his brain. I know I was injured and had to physically recover, but I never suffered quite the same way he did. He once told me to avoid the papers and to never look at the crime-scene photos, and I took his advice. Why would I want those horrific images to become my memories?"

"Rory is smart," she said. "And I love that he and Sadie found each other."

"Rory struggled to move forward. Sadie is helping him," he agreed.

Charity was silent for a moment. "That's my problem. I can't seem to get solid forward momentum, and Jenny once told me it's because at some point in my life I circled the wagons to protect me. But because of that, I've never been able to move on and accomplish the things I want to because I'm still in one spot, wagons circled, rifles drawn, waiting for the next attack." She shrugged. "I was mad at her when she said that, but she's right. It's why I'm still at home. It's why I didn't go to New York to study design. It's why I doubt myself so much."

Quinn pulled her to the side, out of the way of the other skaters. "You played it safe because you had to play it safe, and there's nothing wrong with that. You were doing what you thought was necessary to survive."

"But I'm tired of playing it safe. I want more from life. I love fashion, I love beautiful clothes, I want to have my own business one day, and maybe that's not practical—"

"But why does every choice have to be practical?" he interrupted. "Why not do things because it's just fun?" Quinn gestured to the ice rink and the couples skating. "We're not here because it's practical. We're here because it's fun. I love spending time with you because it feels good to be with you. Is it practical? Probably not. But do I want to be with you as much as I can while I'm here in Montana? Absolutely."

"Why?" she whispered.

"Because you make me happy. Being with you makes me happy. And as we both know, life can be hard, and there are no guarantees, so we have to make the most of every single day we're given."

"Seize the day," she murmured.

"Live every day as if it's your last," he replied.

She felt almost overwhelmed by emotion. She nodded, finding it impossible to speak.

"What do you say we get something warm to drink?" he suggested.

"Good idea," she said, taking the hand he offered and following him off the ice.

They waited in line to buy cups of hot chocolate and Charity laughed when Quinn asked for extra mini marshmallows on his. He glanced at her, eyebrow raised. "Want extra marshmallows on yours?"

She started to shake her head and then changed her mind. "Yes, actually. That would be lovely."

They found a place near the ice to sit, and Quinn drew her close to his hip, his arm around her as they sipped their chocolate and watched others skate.

"I think you need to make yourself a priority," he said after a moment. "Put together a business plan and make your shop a reality. There's no reason you can't have your own business here."

"Oh, are you going to invest in me and Little Teton now?" she teased.

"Maybe."

"I'm not sure fashion and Marietta go hand in hand."

"There is a lot of money in this area. Beautiful clothes are always in demand, and before you tell me that I don't know anything about couture, my great-great-great-aunt, Johanna Douglas, was Marietta's first fashion designer. She had a shop on Main Street named Johanna Design in the 1880's. If she could have a shop, why can't you?"

Charity's mouth opened and then closed. "Is that true?"

"The library has a display of old photographs and you can see a picture of Johanna Douglas in front of her shop with her mother, and her brother, Sinclair Douglas, who was my great-great-great-grandfather."

"That's very cool."

"If a young, Irish immigrant could open up her own shop in frontier Marietta, you can, too."

"Thank you for your confidence," she said, smiling up at him. She felt so happy right now, happy and calm and optimistic. It had been a long time since she felt so optimistic. Maybe it was time to stop being afraid of everything. Maybe it was time to face her fears head-on.

"I haven't been honest with you," she said quietly.

"No?" he said, giving her a quizzical look before stretching out his long legs, and crossing his skates at the ankle.

"No, and I'm sorry about that and I didn't mean to be dishonest with you. I think it happened because I haven't been honest with myself." She looked up into his face, and her eyes met his. Her head felt a bit fuzzy as his gaze locked with hers. "Quinn, I don't think of you as a friend. I'm not even sure what it means to be on your team because if being teammates means being buddies, I don't want that. I won't ever be your drinking buddy or your wingman because it would kill me to go out on a date with you, and not be your date."

He lifted a brow, his expression amused, but he said nothing. Silence stretched, and Charity stirred on the bench, feeling the frantic flutter of butterflies in her middle.

"Are you ready for another confession?" she asked after a moment.

"I think I can handle the shock."

She glanced at him swiftly and he was grinning, and she smiled crookedly, unable to resist him when he smiled at her.

"Go on," he said. "I've braced myself."

"I'm wildly attracted to you."

"Wildly?" he repeated.

She nodded. "Like… yes." She drew another swift, sharp breath, determined to get through this and just lay all her cards on the table. "My feelings aren't easy to manage anymore, either. I thought if we kept things… platonic… I'd be okay around you. But my feelings just keep getting stronger, and I'm beginning to realize they're not going to go away."

"I'm just glad you're figuring out what I already know."

"And what is that?"

"That you're meant to be mine."

"How can you know that when we've had so little actual romance?"

"Every minute I spend with you is romantic."

Heat rushed through her, and her pulse drummed. "And yet we only had that one little kiss in Wyoming."

His broad shoulders shifted. "But it was a good one."

She felt a funny little flutter in her middle and just talking about kissing made her lips tingle. "It was a good kiss. So good that sometimes all I can think about is kissing you again—"

The rest of her words were cut off by his mouth covering hers. His hand cupped her nape, and his thumb stroked her cheek and his lips felt even more amazing than she remembered.

Quinn didn't hurry the kiss either. He took his time, deepening the kiss, parting her lips, and Charity was gone, lost in the pleasure, lost in him.

When he finally lifted his head, her heart pounded and her skin prickled and Charity gazed into his eyes thinking yes, yes, this was the one she'd been waiting for.

CHAPTER NINE

CHARITY WAS AT her desk early Monday morning, a little nervous about the text Sam had sent her late last night, asking her to meet with him early in the morning.

Charity didn't mind coming in early as she'd hoped she'd be able to leave early, too. The ping-pong balls were painted, but Mandy's gown was still just a bolt of shimmering emerald-green satin. She also wanted to make something for herself if she could only figure out what she should wear.

The front door opened and Sam entered the office in a flurry of snow.

"It's a cold one," Sam said, removing his coat.

"The office was freezing this morning. You should be grateful I arrived first, otherwise your teeth would still be chattering."

"Let me pour some coffee and then can you meet me in my office?" he asked.

"I'll be right in."

"Do you know what this is about?" he asked when she took a seat across from his desk.

She shook her head.

"I wish you'd told me things were escalating," he said, picking up a pen and tapping it on his desk. "I don't condone Greg's behavior."

Charity's confusion cleared. "I didn't want to bother you."

"Bother me? Charity, I'm lucky to have you. I'd rather lose him than you."

"Greg is an agent. He makes you money. I don't."

"People love you, though. Greg... not so much." He leaned back in his chair. "I talked to him over the weekend. He understands that he's on thin ice. I don't expect you'll have any more trouble from him."

"That's good." She hesitated. "What did he say when you talked to him?"

"Oh, the usual bluster, but I'm not interested in his excuses. You've been here longer than he has. You have seniority. And I'd be a fool to let you go. Real estate is all about relationships, and customers love you. You make them feel good. That's a gift."

It was one of the nicest things Sam had ever said to her. "Thank you, Sam."

"Which makes me wonder, do you want to do more here? Would you like to become a real estate agent? I'd be happy to cover the cost of classes and exam fees if that's holding you back."

She was touched, but at the same time, his generosity made her feel guilty because she had no desire to become a

Realtor. She knew the long hours it involved, and how competitive it could be and in all fairness, it just didn't interest her that much. "It's been a tough few weeks, and knowing I have you in my corner helps, but Sam, real estate as a career, isn't for me. I hope you don't mind that I'm content as I am—provided Greg gives me space."

"He will."

"How do you know that?"

"Let's just say if I was Greg, I wouldn't mess with Montana diplomacy."

AFTER WORK, CHARITY forced herself to stay home and focus on Amanda's dress even though she was dying to head out to the Gallaghers to see Noel and Quinn. But she'd promised Amanda a dress and she would deliver. The floor-length dress would be made from a stunning emerald-green charmeuse, and she'd designed it with an hourglass shape. The sleeveless gown featured a draped cowl neckline that was just off the shoulder to better frame Mandy's gorgeous face. The slim sheath silhouette gently flared below the hips to puddle at Mandy's feet. The design wasn't vintage but inspired by the 1940s clothing Amanda loved. With her hair pinned up and some pearl drop earrings—or even something sparkly—she'd be the belle of the ball.

Charity began sewing in sixth grade in an effort to make the dreadful hand-me-downs she and Amanda wore more appealing. It took her a couple of years, but she became an expert seamstress, learning to play with hems and seams, shoulders and necklines. She didn't have money to go to a fabric store, and so she haunted the yard sales, picking up garments to remake in one of her own designs.

Charity loved experimenting with patterns, too, testing fabrics and how they'd hold up over time. By the time she was a sophomore in high school, she could sew anything. She made all of Mandy's party and prom dresses at Marietta High, as well as anything else her sister needed, because Charity was determined Amanda should never feel inferior to anyone, for any reason.

Adjusting the lamp over her sewing table, Charity sat down at her sewing machine. As she eased the fabric under the needle she wondered again what she'd wear Saturday. The gown would have to be dramatic and elegant and wildly romantic. She pictured soft. No sequins. Nothing shiny. Nothing overly revealing either.

She could almost see it in her mind's eye—delicate, an overlay of lace, bare shoulders, gleaming skin—but the rest of the details were still vague. Hopefully with a little bit of time the design would come to her as she wanted to look beautiful at Mistletoe and Montana for Quinn.

"I miss Rusty Noel," she texted Quinn from her desk Tuesday afternoon.

He must have been in the middle of something as it took him a little bit to respond. *"I knew you only liked me for my dog."*

She grinned, heart tumbling. She'd fallen hard for him. So hard. *"It's my dog,"* she replied, before adding, *"If it's any consolation, I miss you, too."*

"Come work at my house tonight. That way you can spend the evening with Rusty Noel."

That actually was a great idea. She'd love to be able to spread out her different tree projects, something she couldn't do at her house on Chance Avenue. *"What if I brought something for an early dinner? Could you sneak away for a half hour?"*

"I'll meet you at the house to let you in, but Sawyer warned me that this week is going to be busy so I won't be able to stay long."

"My plan is to be there by four, so I can get there before dark. Also, need your address."

He sent her the address before adding, *"Text me when you take the first turn off. I'll leave the Gallaghers and meet you there."*

IN THE FIVE years he'd owned his Paradise Valley house, Quinn had never invited his family to dinner. Of course they'd come over at different times, but he'd never thrown a party, or hosted a barbecue. He didn't celebrate holidays here and there had never been guests taking advantage of the many guestrooms. Over the years, Alice had asked about his house, hinting she wanted to see it, but he'd never flown her out for a visit, reluctant to let her see what he'd built for his family one day, certain she'd find fault in decisions he'd made.

Quinn wasn't sure what Charity would think of his house. Would she find it was too big, too imposing? Would she wonder who he was trying to impress?

There were times in the planning and building of the house, he'd worried that he was trying too hard, trying to be someone he wasn't. And then he became annoyed with himself because he had the means to build himself any house he wanted, and this was the one he wanted.

Big, sturdy, spacious, comfortable.

The floor-to-ceiling windows and soaring spaces weren't accidental. He wanted the high ceilings and tall windows so light could pour in. He wanted windows that would let him look out, and up. He wanted to see the peaks of the mountains, as well as the sparkling river coursing through the valley floor.

He wanted the heavens for God and his family, and this bit of earth for his heart and home.

But he'd never shared those thoughts with anyone, and he felt almost bashful as he opened the door and invited Charity in. He watched her face as she crossed the threshold, her expression lit up as Rusty raced to greet her and then her eyes widened as she took in the entry and the great room beyond. The interior, like the exterior, had been crafted from wood and stone, but in the living room, the colors were warm, the wood golden in places and chestnut in others.

Quinn carried her boxes and bags of supplies to the dining room table and placed them at one end. "Feel free to spread out," he said. "Use every surface in every room. It's all yours."

"This is a lot of space," she murmured.

"I grew up with a big family," he answered, "but we were crammed into a small ranch house. I thought I'd give my kids more space." The moment he said the words he kicked himself because she'd grown up in a house far smaller than his, but she didn't seem to be bothered. She just nodded thoughtfully, her gaze fixed on the horizon and where the sun had set behind the Gallatins, streaks of pink and lavender painting the sky.

"You probably get a spectacular sunset every night, don't you?" she said.

The sunset might be striking but he couldn't bother to look, too taken by her lovely face and pretty profile. "If I were here," he answered. "Since returning, I've been at the Gallaghers every night at this time."

She glanced at him then and smiled. It wasn't one of her teasing smiles, or nervous smiles. This smile was slow, and warm, and filled with something almost like… appreciation. The effect was dazzling. Her smile made him feel powerful.

"You're doing such a good thing," she said, "helping them out. You have no idea how much I admire you, or respect you—"

"This community has given me so much. It's only right that I give back."

"You're going above and beyond."

"It's hard for me to explain, but this is exactly what I should be doing. Being here, giving back. I needed this."

Something horrific happened on his family's ranch, and yet something beautiful took place in the aftermath.

People came together, and loved hard, and their love made the difference. Love made a difference.

It was why he was here now. For the Gallaghers, yes, but also Charity. She was the one he was meant to be with.

He couldn't explain how he knew, only that he knew it was true. The same way he'd always known that there was a reason he'd been spared that day on the ranch.

"Is there anything else I can bring in from your car?" he asked.

"No, that's everything."

"Then let me show you how the alarm on the house works, and then I'll head back to the Gallaghers."

AFTER QUINN LEFT, Charity watched the last glow of light fade from the horizon and then walked around the house, turning on lights, trying to make herself feel more comfortable. Rusty followed her on her self-guided tour, keeping close to her side.

Quinn's house was lovely. No, lovely wasn't an accurate description. The house was huge, stunning, by far the most luxurious thing she had ever seen. Stone and wood, mammoth rock fireplaces, massive beams, supple leather sofas the color of butterscotch. The kitchen was the size of her family home on Chance Avenue. The landing on the stairs could easily accommodate a bed and dresser. There were six bedrooms and eight bathrooms and views out every window.

She peeked into the master bedroom and it had a big bed to match the soaring ceiling and airy space, and yet it was surprisingly serene. A cream duvet cover. Cream pillow shams. And then folded on the foot of the bed was an antique patchwork quilt edged in a navy velvet.

Charity found the quilt irresistible and crossed the room to examine it more closely. It was all hand stitched and the fabric was worn thin in places but the colors of the silk and wool fabric remained vivid.

She ran her hand over the midnight-blue velvet trim. It felt plush and decadent. She wondered if Quinn ever pulled the quilt up, or if it was merely decorative. There had to be a story to it. She'd love to know the story, and hoped it was his family's and not just an accent piece purchased by his interior designer.

Downstairs again, Charity knew it was time to settle down and work. But she couldn't get comfortable. The house was too polished, too perfect. With the exception of the wreath on the front door, Quinn's house lacked holiday cheer. Fortunately, Charity knew a way to add cheer quickly. She connected her phone to Quinn's Bluetooth speakers and put on her favorite Christmas album and then turned it up loud, singing along with Kelly Clarkson as she laid out the strings of lights on the enormous dining room table. Once the four strings of lights were out, she began attaching the painted ping-pong balls to the miniature white lights. Every third light got a ping-pong ball, and a dollop of superglue to hold the ball in place.

While the glue dried, she laid the pennants in a circle on the huge kitchen island, trying to come up with a pleasing pattern. Blue, green, blue, gold, green…

She stepped back to study the colors. She was short pennants, but the pennant tree skirt needed something. Maybe more color? Or maybe just two colors, maybe she should keep it all the Mariners blue and green? Or maybe she could take a red wool or velvet and mix it in with the blues and green, so blue Mariners pennant, hunter-green Mariners pennant, dark red fabric, and then the blue and green again. If she did that, she wouldn't need more pennants and she could finish the tree skirt tonight. She liked that idea.

Things were coming together. Everything was falling into place. She'd found red, blue, and green glass balls at the Mercantile, and Sadie was selling vintage silver and gold stars in her shop on Main Street. The plastic sleeves had arrived, and she'd filled them with baseball cards from Mr. Gallagher's collection and looped red, blue, and white ribbon at the top of each to create a hanger for the tree. Even if nothing arrived from the Seattle Mariner store, they'd have a beautiful baseball themed tree.

She returned to the lights to check if the ping-pong balls were attached, and when she lifted part of one strand, they stayed in place, glowing like miniature baseballs.

She couldn't help smiling at her handiwork. The lights were adorable.

Rusty lifted his head and whined. Charity glanced out the window. It was dark out. She didn't know what had caught Rusty's attention.

He sat up and barked. Charity glanced toward the windows again, suddenly wishing she'd drawn the tall drapes to cover all that glass.

Then the doorbell rang. Charity glanced from the door to Rusty, who was now standing between her and the door. Charity wasn't exactly scared, but she did feel uneasy.

She muted the music and went to the door, peeked through the peephole, and spotted a woman on the doorstep. She was young and very pretty, with long brown hair, a thick fur coat, and knee-high boots. She also had two huge suitcases with her.

Charity used the security system's intercom. "Hi, can I help you?"

"I'm looking for Quinn Douglas's place. The GPS brought me here, but maybe it was wrong."

Charity's stomach fell. "You got it right. This is his house."

"In that case, would you please let me in? It's freezing out here!"

"I'm sorry, I don't know who you are and Quinn didn't mention he had any visitors coming."

"I'm not a visitor," the woman answered indignantly. "I'm Alice Sterling, his girlfriend."

His girlfriend.

Charity's legs went weak and her insides lurched. "Just a moment," she said unsteadily, hands shaking as she attempted to turn off the alarm to open the door but she got it wrong the first time and had to try a second time before getting it to turn off so she could open the door.

Alice looked Charity up and down before pulling one suitcase in. She left the other on the doorstep and then closed the door. "Quinn can get that one later. It's just his baseball stuff."

Charity watched Alice walk through the entry and on into the great room. "It's actually nicer than I imagined," she said, almost under her breath. She continued her exploring, brazenly walking from the living room to the dining room where she paused to study the strings of baseball lights.

"Cute," Alice said, giving Charity a cool smile. "It seems as if you have been working hard on this project for the tree auction."

Charity didn't answer, far too uncomfortable to think of a single thing to say. Rusty sat next to her feet, his big warm body touching her legs.

Alice continued into the kitchen where she studied the pennant tree skirt. "The gold looks drab with the blue and green," she said, before glancing up at Charity again and giving her another cool smile. "But I think it's a very clever idea. It will be fun to see it all come together. I expect Quinn's memorabilia will raise a significant amount of money. At any rate, I'm planning on bidding it up." She went to Charity. "But don't tell Quinn. He hates is when I spend money on him."

"Well, it wouldn't actually be money spent on him, it's a fund-raiser," Charity finally said, finding her voice at last. "All money raised will be going to help others."

Alice gently pulled apart the pennant skirt and stacked the pennants into a pile. "I'm worried you're going to get hurt. You seem very sweet. But Quinn's a complicated man. As much as he wants to belong here, he doesn't. Ask him some time if you don't believe me. He feels like an outsider. He doesn't fit in, and yes, he loves his family, but Montana represents his past, not his future." She lifted the top pennant and flashed it at Charity. "His home is in Seattle now. Seattle gives him a different identity. He can get lost there, and forget his grief."

Alice returned the pennant to the stack and circled the island, studying everything. "This place honestly isn't what I expected. He built it before we met. It's like a dream house. Something you'd see in *Architectural Digest*. Now, I'd expect this from my dad. Dad is all about trying to impress people. I didn't think Quinn wanted that, and yet when you look at this place you realize he needs people to think he's doing okay."

"He is doing okay," Charity said quietly.

"But he's not. It's an act. A façade, if you will. Something he projects because it's what people expect of him. Quinn's the good Douglas. He's the positive, nice-guy one. And unfortunately, he has to be that person here in Montana. He has to be that way for all of you... just so you can be okay with what happened on his ranch that day."

Charity fought a wave of anger. "That's not true. No one expects that of him, or wants it from him. People love him because he's one of us, not because he's a baseball player, or a survivor from the ranch massacre."

"If you say so." Alice shrugged and pulled out a barstool from the island and sat down. Her thick fur coat fell open and revealed her very slender figure. "I love Quinn. I have loved him from the moment I met him, and he loves me. We've had a bumpy few months, but it's not the first time. We'll get through this. We always do."

"I'm not sure what you want me to say," Charity said after a moment.

"Just be careful. As I said, you seem very sweet—"

"I'm not that sweet."

Alice's lips curved into a hard smile. "Good, because I'm not sweet at all."

"I gathered that," Charity answered calmly, even though she was a panicked mess underneath. She felt foolish and naked and terribly exposed. She didn't want to be here anymore, but she wasn't about to let Alice chase her off.

She went to the dining room table and checked on the strings of lights with the painted ping-pong balls. As she lifted a second string, a little ball fell off and bounced onto the ground. Charity retrieved it and finding her glue, reattached the ball more securely. She could feel Alice's gaze on her, and it felt like she was burning a hole through her back but Charity refused to rush.

Quinn had said he and Alice were finished. Quinn had said he was single and available and just because Alice was here, didn't mean Alice could just take Quinn back.

"I hope you brought the bobble head dolls," Charity said, giving Alice a smile. "Because they'll look adorable on the tree."

"If you scratch them, they'll lose their value."

"I won't, and I'll be as careful with their boxes as I have been with everything else." Charity tapped one of the baseball cards in the plastic sleeve. It was from Quinn's rookie year and he looked like a kid. "I just feel so lucky to have grown up with Quinn," she said. "We both love Montana so much."

"I know what you're doing," Alice said, approaching her. Her glance fell onto the rookie card and she studied it a moment before looking up at Charity. "It won't work. You're going to lose."

"Lose what?" Charity countered. "This is my home. This is where I live. Quinn's sister McKenna is one of my close friends. Rory, Quinn's brother, is married to another one of my best friends. Quinn isn't a baseball player to me. He's not someone famous. Or someone to parade about, thankful he makes me look good. He's just Quinn Douglas, and someone I love."

Charity slipped all the plastic protected cards into a box, and then topped them with the strings of lights before gathering her purse and coat. "I'll pick up the things you brought tomorrow. Thanks for hand carrying them out. Have a good night."

Rusty Noel followed Charity to the front door and whined as it became clear he wasn't going with her. She felt terrible about everything and she was just about to fall apart, but she couldn't do that in here, not with Alice hovering like a hawk.

Charity juggled her boxes and bags and gave Rusty Noel scratch beneath his chin. "See you soon, Noel," she whispered, before letting herself out and closing the door.

It wasn't until she was in her car on Highway 89 that her calm cracked. She hated leaving Alice in Quinn's house. She didn't want Alice anywhere near Quinn but for all Charity knew, Quinn wanted her there.

For all she knew, Quinn had invited Alice out.

For all she knew, Quinn hadn't completely severed ties with Alice, which meant Alice had good reason to be smug.

CHAPTER TEN

S HE WASN'T PICKING up.

At first Quinn thought Charity might just be busy with one of her projects, but as the evening went on and she failed to respond to his calls, or his texts asking her to check in, his unease grew. This silence wasn't like her. Was she okay? Had something happened? Immediately, he thought of Greg and his worry intensified.

He didn't like thinking about what took place on his ranch twenty-one years ago, but of course the violence had affected him. It was why he had a sophisticated security system for the house. The house wasn't as isolated as the Douglas ranch had been, but there weren't any close neighbors. No one to keep track of coming and goings.

Every ten to fifteen minutes he'd glance at his phone to see if a text came in from her. Finally he couldn't handle it anymore. He went to Rory and told him he had to run home to check on something, but he should be back right away. Rory wasn't worried. Quinn lived close. Pulling up to his house, Quinn spotted an unfamiliar car in his driveway. He also noticed that Charity's Subaru was gone.

A big burgundy hard-sided suitcase stood on the front porch near the door. Quinn recognized the suitcase. Alice had an entire set of luggage like this one. He knew, because he'd bought the set for her last Christmas.

The fight or flight anxiety began to ease, replaced by dread. Quinn was beginning to get a clear idea of what happened, and it wasn't good.

He let himself into the house and spotted the other matching suitcase in the hall. He glanced around, looking for Alice and Rusty.

He found Alice in the kitchen, opening a bottle of wine. She'd located two glasses from one of the cabinets and flashed him a smile. "Hey, handsome, I wondered when you'd get here."

"I'm not staying," he said. "I've got to get back to the Gallaghers." He frowned as she filled the glasses, thinking the house didn't feel right. Everything was too quiet. "Where did you get the wine from?"

"I brought it from home. Your favorite winery," she said, turning the bottle to show off the label.

He glanced around again, and then realized why everything felt off. "Where's Rusty?"

"Rusty?"

"My dog."

"Why would you get a dog? You're coming back home soon." Her lips pursed. "And if you really, really want a dog, we're going to get a puppy that we pick out together."

Quinn couldn't even answer that, unable to string together sentences that would be polite. He whistled, and then called Rusty's name.

Alice handed him a wineglass. "He's in the laundry room," she said. "He was scratching at the front door and it was annoying."

Quinn set the glass down on the counter harder than he intended. "I don't know what you're doing here," he said tersely, "but you can't stay." And then he headed for the laundry room to let Rusty out.

Alice followed him slowly, wineglass in hand. "It's almost eight. The nearest town is thirty minutes away. Where do you expect me to go at this time of night?"

"To the nearest town and it's not thirty minutes. It's only twenty minutes to Marietta, and twenty-five to the Graff Hotel which should have plenty of room for you this time of year," he answered, opening the door. The laundry room was dark. He flipped on the light and Rusty immediately came to him, and pushed his head into Quinn's hand. Poor dog.

And then he thought of Charity and his chest grew tighter, and harder, and he could only imagine what she was feeling right now. He turned around and faced Alice. "Why are you here?"

"I brought out the things you wanted," she answered, her tone excessively reasonable.

This was how she liked to play ball. She would act like she was the calm, rational one and he was impractical and unrealistic.

He ground his teeth together, battling to control his anger. "What did you say to Charity?"

"I wondered what her name was."

"Alice?"

Her slender shoulder lifted and fell. "Nothing bad and nothing that wasn't true."

"What does that mean?"

"It means that I love you. And I thought it important she knew."

He swore silently, aware that Alice had just turned his relationship with Charity inside out because confidence wasn't Charity's strong suit. Greg had done a number on her self-esteem and Alice's appearance had to have rattled Charity.

He needed to see her. He needed to do damage control, fast. "I have to go," he said. "And so do you. I'll put your suitcases back in your car and you can check in at the Graff, or whatever Marietta hotel you choose, but I strongly encourage you to be on a flight tomorrow because I won't be seeing you tomorrow, or any other time in the future."

"There's no reason to kick me out, Quinn. This house is huge. There are plenty of bedrooms—"

"No."

"I'm not asking to share a bed with you, baby. I just think it's silly to send me all that way back to that strange little town—"

"Alice, stop. You're not endearing yourself to me. In fact, every word you say just makes everything worse. So you need to go now before I say things I'll regret."

"Like what?"

"Like you're manipulative and spoiled and selfish." He paused, lifted a brow. "Should I go on?"

"That was harsh," she whispered.

"I warned you."

"You promised we'd always be friends."

"Friends respect each other." He walked down the hall toward the spacious entry. "Which suitcase has my things in it?"

"The one outside," she said, voice low.

He brought the case in, opened it, and pulled out everything that looked like it belonged to him, and then closed the case, and set it on its wheels next to the other one. "Ready?" he said, curtly.

"No." And then she saw his expression and sighed. "Yes. But, Quinn, please don't be so mad at me. I'm doing what I can to protect us."

"But there is no us," he said firmly. "There hasn't been an us for years."

"We only broke up in July."

"I hadn't been happy for a long time."

She knocked away a tear with her knuckled fist. "Are you happy now?"

"I am. I love her, Alice."

"But you've only just returned to Montana."

"I know, but she's the one I've been waiting for."

CHARITY SAT ON her bed and played the voice mail messages Quinn had left for her.

"I went to the house to check on you and discovered Alice there and you gone. It's not what you think. I do not want her here. She's no longer at my house. Please call me back."

And then, *"Charity, why won't you respond? I know you're upset but let me explain. We're supposed to be friends. Friends hear each other out."*

And then the last, *"Charity, it's almost nine, I'm wrapping up here at the Gallaghers and on my way to Marietta. I'll be at your house in twenty-five minutes."*

He'd left that last message over an hour ago, and she'd waited for him to come, but he hadn't. She'd fixed her hair and changed her clothes and put on fresh makeup so he wouldn't know she'd been crying, and then he'd been a no show.

This was exactly why she hadn't wanted to fall in love. She hadn't wanted to be hurt and disappointed again. Growing up, her life had been filled with hurt and disappointment. She was tired of being less than, tired of emotions that left her feeling broken.

Fighting back fresh tears, Charity changed into her pajamas and prepared for bed. She wasn't going to be able to sleep though. She couldn't remember when she last felt so miserable.

The last few weeks had been amazing and she'd felt so much hope and happiness. And fun. With Quinn she'd had fun. And he'd been a friend. They'd talked about so many things and she'd come to trust him. Which was why she'd dared to hope. And dream.

Her phone rang twenty minutes later. She let it ring another time before picking it up off her bedside table.

Quinn.

A lump filled her throat as she looked at his name on her phone.

For a split second she considered not answering and then realized she was too exhausted to play games. If it was going to end, then let it end cleanly right now. She couldn't do the back and forth. She couldn't handle another Greg situation.

"Hello?" she answered, her voice still rough from her earlier tears.

"Charity, Noel is missing," Quinn said bluntly. "That's why I'm not there. I've been out driving Highway 89 and all the back roads, looking for him. I'd hoped to have found him by now, as I didn't want to worry you, but since I haven't, I needed to tell you. I don't know how he got out of the house, and I'm sorry—"

"I'm going to go look, too," she said, jumping out bed. "I'll start driving around Marietta."

"I'm on my way to Marietta now. Why don't I just pick you up? I should be at your house soon."

"I'll be ready," she said simply, pulling warm clothes on instead.

They drove for an hour, up and down Main Street, up and down Church, up and down Bramble, up and down every single side street. Nothing. No sign of a big red dog, or any dog, anywhere.

It was after midnight when Quinn drove Charity back home. They'd refrained from discussing anything personal while searching for Rusty, but now that Quinn was pulling down her street, Charity summoned the courage to broach the other issue very much on her mind. "Alice," she said quietly.

"I'm sorry I wasn't there when she arrived," he said.

"It wouldn't have changed anything," she answered, trying very hard to keep her emotions under control, "because it doesn't change the facts."

"And just what are those facts?"

"She claims she's your girlfriend—"

"She's not."

"She says she is."

"She's wrong and she deliberately mislead you," he retorted grimly, pulling up in front of her house and shifting into park. "Don't believe anything she told you."

Wasn't that what Greg had said, too? For her not to believe the gossip? For her to listen to him? And yet Greg had played her, and played her...

Was Quinn just another Greg?

Charity closed her eyes and held her breath as she pressed her fingers to her brow bone. Her head thumped. Her heart hurt. She was devastated they hadn't found Noel and still shaken from her encounter with Alice and confused by everything happening with Quinn. "I don't want to do this with you right now," she whispered. "I'm so tired I can't think straight."

"Look at me, Charity," he said urgently. "There is nothing between Alice and me. I give you my word. I swear—"

"But she's *here*. And she seems pretty certain you two are still a couple, or about to be a couple again."

"She's having a hard time accepting that we're over."

Charity blinked hard, trying to hold back the tears. "Or maybe you're not really over. Maybe you're still with her, or meant to be with—"

"*No.*"

"I wish I could believe you," she said tightly, the air trapped in her lungs. She hadn't wanted to cry in front of Alice, and now she didn't want to cry in front of Quinn. She had to cling to a shred of self-respect. "I want to believe you, but my head is mocking my heart, telling me to wise up and see what's really going on."

"Nothing is going on. Charity, I've never lied to you. I've always been truthful."

"Well, with the exception of you being Douglas Quincy."

"You're not innocent there either. You pretended to be

Tricia Thorpe, but I've never held that against you."

She didn't answer. She couldn't answer.

From the corner of her eye, she saw him flex a gloved hand against the steering wheel. "I never kept Alice a secret," he said in a low voice. "From the beginning I told you about her, and shared how it was a relationship that didn't work. Everything I said was true—"

"Then why is she here?" The words burst out, sharp and loud. "Why is she staying at your place?"

"She's not. I've kicked her out. Sent her away."

"Where did she go?"

"I don't know. I suggested the Graff, but she might have decided to keep driving on to Bozeman."

"If she's at the Graff I might have the chance to see her tomorrow. That would be fun."

"Now you're just being sarcastic." But his tone was mild and he seemed to be fighting a smile.

"Of course you think this is funny. But you should have seen her, swanning around your house, telling me how much she loved you and how she seemed to be the only one who truly understood you."

"If I thought she understood me, we'd be together, but we're not. We haven't been together, in any size, shape or form since July fifth."

"And yet she's *here*. She said you needed your sports memorabilia and you asked her to fly them out."

"I asked her to mail them."

"Maybe it's time you introduced her to the US Postal Service." Charity sat for a moment, trying to organize her chaotic feelings, but her head wasn't working. Her thoughts were wild and this conversation was just going in circles.

Was it only two days ago that they'd skated at Miracle Lake? Was it just two days ago that she'd confessed her true feelings? If only she could take that afternoon back. If only she could somehow protect her heart.

Quinn wasn't safe.

Quinn was just more instability and heartache.

"I need to get to bed," she said, reaching for the truck's door handle. "Please let me know if Rusty Noel is there when you get home, or if he shows up later. I don't care what time it is."

"I promise," Quinn answered, opening his truck door to come around and open hers. He gave her a hand, assisting her out. He walked with her to the front door. "Charity, things are going to be okay."

She wished she could be so sure. She dug her key out of her purse and gave him a troubled look as she unlocked the front door. "Good night, Quinn."

He kissed the top of her head. If he felt her stiffen and pull away, he gave no indication. "Good night, Charity."

QUINN DROVE BACK to Paradise Valley feeling worse than he had in a very long time.

Things had been going well, so well, until tonight.

He'd felt good being back in Montana. He'd felt happy... contented... at peace.

He'd felt at home.

Charity was the one who'd made him feel at home, too. She made everything feel right.

She was the missing piece. He wanted her in his life, and he still firmly believed she was meant to be in his life, and yet it was a shock to realize how fragile her trust in him was, and how quickly Alice had damaged Charity's sense of self.

Charity was the one he wanted. In her eyes, he could see the life he wanted... he could see the future he wanted. But she had to want it, too.

She had to trust him, and she had to have more faith in herself. He knew her childhood had left her scarred and scared, but at some point, you had to let the past go, or it would haunt you forever.

Could she do that?

Could she learn to believe in him....and them?

Their relationship wouldn't survive if they both didn't fight for it. One person couldn't do all the heavy lifting. There had to be some kind of glue to keep them together when hard times came, because hard times would come. Hopefully, he'd never have to live through another tragedy. Hopefully, he'd never lose to violence anyone else he loved, but faith was still required, for situations large and small. Faith in God, faith in others, and faith in one's self.

Quinn didn't care that Charity didn't like sports or fol-low baseball, but he cared very much about her opinion of him. He'd devoted his life to his sport, and to working with youth, and trying to use his platform to help others. He was a strong person, and he lived life with conviction, but every now and then he needed support. He could use Charity's support now.

It was a long night, and Quinn slept badly. He tossed and turned and then left bed at four thirty to make coffee and watch the news.

It was just six when his phone rang, with an early call from Sawyer.

"Sorry for the crack of dawn call, but I figured you'd be worried. Your dog is here," Sawyer said. "We woke up to find him asleep in the barn. Not sure how he found a way in, but Jenna discovered him curled up on a wool blanket by the cash register."

Quinn exhaled with relief. "Thank goodness. I'll call Charity and let her know. We drove around until midnight looking for him."

"I'm not sure why he came here, unless he was looking for you, and thought you might be here."

"I should have brought him back with me last night, af-ter I went over to my house. An ex-girlfriend had stopped by. She wasn't very nice to him. Rusty Noel must've been spooked."

"Rusty Noel?"

"His name is Rusty, but Charity still thinks of him as Noel, so Rusty Noel it is."

"You do know that sounds like Rusty Nail, don't you?"

Quinn laughed, and then his laugh faded. "Hey, do you think your man Rob can handle opening this morning without me? I'd like to come get the dog and take him to Charity. I'm sure Sam won't mind if the dog camps out by her desk today, and I know she'd be thrilled to have him."

"No problem at all. I'm already more mobile than I was. I was thinking I'd try to get out there today and lend a hand. I can't show trees but I could work the cash register. So no rush. Take your time."

NEITHER SAM NOR Greg was at the office when Charity arrived the next morning. Charity was glad.

As she made a pot of coffee, she blinked hard, her eyes gritty. She'd cried more than she'd slept last night, and this morning after she'd showered, she'd applied ice packs to her eyes to reduce the puffiness.

She'd cried over Alice's appearance at Quinn's house. She'd cried with worry over Noel being missing. She'd cried because she was worn out and filled with insecurity, and now that her insecurities had been set loose, they were tearing her apart.

She'd never felt good enough and all it took was one look at poised, polished Alice Sterling to realize Charity had never been Quinn's type. He was a city guy. He wanted a poised, confident, sophisticated woman. Charity wasn't that woman.

Heartsick, she carried her cup of coffee to her desk and sat down, turning on her computer, and checking her email. She couldn't focus on the emails, though. Her thoughts jumped wildly from Noel to Alice to Quinn and then back to Alice, who was most likely enjoying a latte at the Graff right now.

Just picturing Alice at the Graff made Charity want to throw up.

Charity was staring out into the front window, lost in a fog of misery, when she spotted a very familiar man outside, walking a very familiar dog.

Quinn. Noel.

Noel.

She jumped to her feet and rushed toward the front door even as the door opened and Quinn brought the retriever inside. Noel's tail thumped as Charity gave him a big hug. His coat was cold but he looked well and happy.

"Where did you find him?" Charity asked, glancing up at Quinn.

"He'd gone to the Gallaghers last night. Sawyer and Jenna found him this morning."

"I'm so glad he's safe. I've been so worried. Maybe I can stop crying now." Her voice cracked and just like that, tears filled her eyes again.

"How about he stays with you today? I'll head down to

the Mercantile and get him a dog bed and he can lay next to your desk."

"I'd have to ask Sam," she said.

"I've already called him. He doesn't have a problem with it."

Her throat squeezed closed and her heart knotted and she wished they could go back to Sunday where she'd felt so happy, and safe, with him. "In that case, great."

"While I'm out, can I get you a mocha from Java Café? Maybe one of their delicious breakfast sandwiches?" he asked.

She shook her head, tears stinging her eyes and sat back down at her desk. "I'm good. Just the bed for Noel. Thank you."

"Charity," he said quietly, "you're getting yourself worked up over nothing."

Her shoulders rose and fell. "But it's not nothing, not to me."

"Alice isn't a threat."

"You say that, but she's still very much in the picture." She finally forced herself to look up at him and meet his gaze. "I don't trust her. And maybe because of that, I can't trust you."

"Ouch," he murmured.

She saw him flinch and it just made her feel worse. She wasn't even sure who she was angry at anymore, only that what had seemed so good now seemed like an illusion. "She's not my girlfriend, Quinn," she said fiercely. "She's yours, and she's here, in my town, telling me how she's the only one that knows you and understands you and that basically, at the end of this, she's going to be the last woman standing."

"Only if you let her be."

"What does that mean?"

"Don't let her win."

"Maybe if I was a sports fan your sports analogy would make more sense."

He lifted a brow, and he didn't look impressed. "Let me lay it out for you then," he said, his deep voice impatient. "I'm a professional athlete. I play baseball. My world is a tough world, and it's competitive. My job performance is written up nightly in the paper. My team gets discussed in detail on national TV. If I have a good night, it's talked about. If I have a bad night, it's talked about. To make it more complicated, there are women out there who are groupies, and overzealous fans. These women throw themselves at the players. They exist on the fringes of all professional sports, and they're desperate to snare a player of their own. They want to be part of the action, and the money, and the lifestyle, and they go to great lengths to get attention."

"Are you saying Alice is one of them?"

"No, but she knew about them, and we could talk about the distractions out there, and that's what I want us to be able to do. We should be able to talk about our feelings without worrying that someone is going to fall apart or run away, and I know you're afraid of change, but I'm not going to hurt you, or lie to you. You are too important to me."

"It takes time to build trust."

"But it's also hard to trust others if you can't trust yourself." He gave her a long look. "Or love yourself."

She flinched. "That's rough. I didn't expect that from you."

"We're friends. We're supposed to tell each other the truth."

"Then let me tell you a truth—I'm not tough like you. I will never be as tough as you."

"No, maybe not, but that doesn't mean you can't toughen up, because I think you should. You let losers and schmucks bruise you, and you doubt the people you should trust."

She jerked her chin up and stared at him, quietly furious with him for reading her so well. He wasn't saying anything new. She'd heard all this—and more—from Amanda and Jenny.

"Growing a thicker skin will only help protect your heart," he added. "It won't change who you are. But it will help you survive in this world of ours."

"Maybe I don't like your baseball world anymore."

"Sweetheart, everything I'm talking about has taken place here in Montana. You're being hurt by idiots in this town.

You're struggling to survive in sweet, little Marietta."

She lifted her chin even higher. "I don't think we're friends at all."

Quinn gave his head a faint shake, his expression rueful. "You're not getting rid of me that easily. We're friends. We're more than friends. You're my girl. You're someone I love. And I still love you, even though you're seriously ticked off with me."

"I don't think I want to be on your team anymore."

"Tough. You don't get to just quit like that."

Charity didn't answer, she couldn't, and after a long, tense, miserable minute, Quinn walked out.

CHAPTER ELEVEN

I T WAS A terrible morning. Charity's hands shook so much that she couldn't even type without constant missed keystrokes.

She tried answering the phone but nearly burst into tears.

Sam pulled her into his office, wondering what Greg had done now, and she'd been forced to explain that this wasn't Greg, but Quinn. Or rather Quinn's ex-girlfriend, Alice Sterling, who was in town, staying at the Graff.

By noon, Charity was beyond wiped out. Legs shaking, she put on a heavy coat, leashed Noel and walked him over to Amanda's hair salon. She told Noel to sit in the corner of the waiting room, and then went in search of her sister.

Amanda was at the shampoo bowl, washing a client's hair, but after taking a look at Charity's face, she called one of her assistants to take over. "Finish rinsing, add the deep conditioner, massage in well, wrap in plastic, put her under the dryer for fifteen minutes and then shampoo again. After the final rinse, come get me, okay?"

Amanda dragged Charity to the small back bedroom used by the estheticians but unoccupied at the moment.

"What's happened?" Amanda said, sitting down on the corner of the treatment bed, and patting the space next to her. "We have a solid eighteen minutes. Talk to me."

"His girlfriend is here." Just saying the words made Charity's chest hurt. "Alice Sterling. She's here in Marietta, at the Graff, probably ordering lunch right now in the president's suite." Charity fought tears. Her voice cracked. "Mandy, why is this happening again?"

"This is a totally different situation. Quinn isn't seeing her anymore. She's his ex."

"But they're still in touch. They talk all the time. She's always texting him. Apparently she has a closet of his stuff."

"I think it's admirable that Quinn can stay friends with his ex-girlfriends. I always thought it was sad that you and Joe couldn't be friends. The fact that he cut you off completely after the breakup hurt you more than the breakup itself."

"At least Joe didn't have anyone else!"

"I don't think Quinn is seeing her."

"Then why is she here? And why did she tell me all these weird things about him? Why did she say that I seemed sweet and she hated to see me hurt? Why tell me that they're going to end up together, and that this is just a temporary blip?"

"Did she really say all that?"

Charity nodded. "And so much more."

"She's making a big play for him, Charity. She's fighting

for him. *You* have her scared."

"She knows nothing about me."

"She knows enough to be here and make a stand." Amanda nudged her sister with her shoulder. "Take a page from her book. Have some balls. Stand up to her. Fight for Quinn. You didn't love Greg, so Meghan wasn't a big deal. But you really care about Quinn, and I know you're afraid, but now's the time to fight. Don't let Alice waltz in, not on your turf, and take away your guy. This is Marietta, Montana. Show her what a Montana girl is made of. And show that Montana boy why you're the right one for him."

Charity bit her lip, her insides churning. "I don't know how to fight," she said, voice strangled. "I don't."

"Not true. You fight for others all the time. You're incredibly generous. But you don't give yourself any love."

Charity flashed to what Quinn had said this morning and it made her cringe. "Are you going to recommend a self-help book next?" she demanded darkly.

"Maybe." Amanda wrapped her arm around her sister's shoulder, and brought her head close. "You're not the only one," she whispered. "We have all struggled with this. We all have terrible self-esteem. But it's not our fault and it doesn't have to be this way. You can fight this fear, you know. You just need to come out swinging and believe that you deserve a really wonderful person, because you to do. Charity, you're my favorite person in the world. I wouldn't adore you so much if you weren't a really amazing person. And I'm not just saying that because you're my sister. I'm saying it because I know you, and I love you, and it's made me so upset to see you date all these terrible guys. It's like that verse in the Bible about throwing pearls before swine."

Amanda released her but she kept a hand on her sister's knee. "You, my gorgeous Charity, are a pearl. You're a rare, wonderful jewel. Demand more, demand more from men and life, and when you find the one you really, truly want, and really, truly love, don't just let him go. *Fight.*"

"Quinn is famous and gorgeous and successful. He could have any woman in the world. He'll tire of me—"

"No! Love doesn't work that way. You and Joe gave up on each other. Maybe it was timing. Maybe you both were too young, but Quinn isn't a kid. He's midthirties, independently wealthy, and established in his career. He knows what he wants in life, and he seems to want you." Amanda squeezed her knee. "Do you really want to push him away?"

"*No.*"

"But I don't have your confidence. I wish I did. I wish I wasn't ashamed of myself."

"Ashamed of what?"

"Everything! Mandy, I'm thirty and I've achieved nothing. I didn't pursue fashion and design. I didn't even apply to Parsons because I didn't think I had a chance."

"You keep calling yourself a failure. You keep blaming yourself for not taking risks. But you did take risks. You took huge risks. You gave up your dreams to take care of me and

Mom and Dad. You are the ultimate caretaker, and that's not what cowards do. It's what brave people do."

Charity glanced away, tears blinding her.

"Don't think I'm not aware of all the times you put yourself on the outside of the bed so that Dad couldn't reach me when he was drunk. Don't think I don't know why you wouldn't go to New York. It's because it would mean leaving me home alone with them. I know who you are, Charity, and it's brave and strong and so full of love that it makes me feel unworthy."

Charity dashed away a tear. "*Stop.*"

"You're my best friend, but also my protector. You've made it your life mission to be sure I was okay, and I'm okay. I'm better than okay. I'm really, truly happy. And now it's time for you to be really, truly happy too."

McKenna stopped by Melk Realty late Monday afternoon to pick up Noel and drive him back to Quinn. She had all the kids in her car and they screamed in delight when Noel joined them in the back seat. Noel, for his part, just lay down and accepted the attention as if that was the reaction he'd expected. He really was such a good dog.

"Thank you for driving him back to Quinn," Charity said, careful to avoid mentioning that anything was amiss between her and Quinn as McKenna adored her big brother.

"We're taking dinner to the guys at the tree farm," she

said, nodding toward the noisy crew in the back seat before giving Charity a frazzled smile. "I keep telling myself this is fun but, right now, I could use a long hot bath without a kidlet in sight."

"Has Trey been at the Gallaghers today?"

"Half day. He came in midafternoon so Rory could go help Sadie haul a tree to a client's house she is decorating."

"Rory's happy, isn't he?" Charity said, hating the wistful note she heard in her voice.

McKenna nodded. "Very happy." And then she hesitated. "And until this week, I would have said the same thing for Quinn." She opened the door to her car and then gave Charity a meaningful glance. "And you two need to sort this out soon because I'm happy to chauffeur this dog to Quinn today, but this shouldn't be an ongoing thing. You guys need to be grown-ups and talk." McKenna waved goodbye, closed her door, and backed out carefully onto Main Street.

Charity watched McKenna's car disappear, hating how horrendous she felt. McKenna was right. This couldn't continue. But Charity didn't know how to make things right with Quinn when Alice was still looming large in the background.

"Don't make me be the one to say it."

Greg's voice caught her off guard, and Charity jumped. "What was that?" she asked, turning around on the sidewalk to face him.

"Come on. Don't make me have to spell this out for you.

I'm not on your team, and I'm not on Quinn's team, but Charity, you are being clueless."

She stiffened and folded her arms across her chest. "What do you want, Greg?"

"I'm trying to help you."

"You've *never* tried to help me."

He grimaced. "That's fair. You make a good point. But putting aside our disastrous relationship, don't let Alice Sterling tie you up in knots."

"How do you know about her?"

"I heard you talking to Sam about her, and I recognized the name. The Sterlings are big in commercial real estate. Her dad, Leo, owns tons of luxury properties and resorts all across the country."

"Your point being?"

"Alice is accustomed to getting what she wants. Don't let her railroad you. Go see her. Sitting around being upset accomplishes nothing. *Do* something about it."

Charity gave Greg a wary look. "After what we've been through, I'm not sure I should listen to your advice."

"If I were you, I'd feel the same way." He sighed and ran a hand through his dark hair. "I'm sorry for how things turned out between us. I was arrogant and a jerk and I treated you badly. I don't feel good about that, and I kind of ruined things for me here in Marietta, too."

She arched an eyebrow. "Did Sam make you say that?"

"Yes. No. Let's face it, I screwed things up for myself

here and I've told Sam that I'm thinking of returning to Omaha. Sam thinks it's probably a good move if I have an opportunity there."

"Next time just be nicer, and have more integrity when you date."

"I think I will take your advice."

She gave him a rueful smile. "And I'll think about yours."

Charity did, too. She thought about Greg's advice all evening as she finished Amanda's dress for the Mistletoe and Montana fund-raiser. Maybe Greg was right. Maybe it was time to confront her fears—namely, Alice—and have a conversation, which meant a visit to the Graff Hotel was in order.

The next morning she stopped by the hotel on her way to work, and approached the front desk asking if they could please connect her to Alice Sterling's room.

The front desk receptionist said there was no one by that name at the hotel. "We did have a guest here Tuesday night by that name, but the guest departed early Wednesday."

Charity's first thought was one of relief—Alice was gone—and then a second thought came, and it was far more disquieting. Had Alice returned to Quinn's?

She felt nauseous as she returned to her car, and drove the three blocks to work. She hated the second thought and, truthfully, she didn't think Alice was at Quinn's. She thought Alice had probably gone home. Charity suspected that everything Quinn had told her was correct.

Her sister's words came back to haunt her.

Quinn wasn't the problem. She was.

THURSDAY MORNING QUINN sent Charity a text that he was slammed that morning and couldn't get the dog to her, but she was welcome to come pick him up, or stop by the Gallaghers later to see him.

Charity read the text several times, telling herself not to read anything into the message, and yet felt anxious all over again. Her stomach had been in knots all week. She hadn't been able to eat much since Tuesday night and it didn't help that she and Quinn weren't speaking. This silence between them reminded her so much of the breakup with Joe, and how when things fell apart it all just ended.

She didn't want this to end with Quinn. In her heart of hearts, she was still so crazy about him, which was why she was keeping her distance. She was afraid. Afraid of rejection. Afraid of his silence. Afraid he'd soon disappear. She was simply afraid, period.

As she went through the motions of working, Charity found herself wondering if part of the reason things had ended so badly with Joe was due to her... and the way she handled hurt and conflict. Had Charity contributed to the problem by not communicating better?

Was it possible even that she'd been the problem?

Amanda certainly made it sound as if she was the problem now, because Charity didn't fight for what she wanted... whether it was a relationship or a career. Instead she gave up. Became a defeatist.

Was it true?

CHARITY LEFT WORK a half hour early to go home and finish the final details on Amanda's dress and then drove it over to Tyler and Amanda's house. Amanda was still at the hair salon but Tyler was home and he took the dress, promising to hang it up straight away in Amanda's closet.

Charity thanked him and started back down the front walkway.

"Do you remember when Amanda and I had our falling out?" he called to her, stopping her midway down the front walk.

She paused and turned around.

"You were instrumental in helping us get back together," he added. "If it wasn't for you, I'm not sure we would've gotten back together, at least not when we did."

Charity's shoulders lifted and fell. "You guys were so good together."

"Just like you and Quinn are good together."

"I'm having a hard time," she admitted. "Quinn and I haven't talked in days."

"So talk to him."

"And what do I say? That I've been wrong about everything? That I'm just a coward with terrible self-esteem issues?"

"That's probably a good start."

"Just a start?"

Tyler came down the steps, walking to her. "And then you add the really important stuff. Like how much you care about him, and how much you've missed him." He smiled at her. "Basic stuff, but still really good to hear stuff."

She glanced away. "He's a professional baseball player," she said in a small voice. "He has groupies and everything."

Tyler's laughter rang out. She shot him an accusing glance. He shrugged. "Sorry," he said, lips twitching, "but the way you said groupies was funny."

"It's not funny, though. Women *throw* themselves at him."

"But he doesn't want them. He wants you."

"His career terrifies me."

"His career is his job, not yours."

"Then what do I do?"

"Just love him. That's all he wants from you."

The knot in her chest grew, making it hard to breathe. "I haven't heard from him in days other than brief, awkward texts about the dog."

"Have you reached out to him?"

She shook her head.

Tyler shrugged. "Maybe he's waiting for you to reassure

him that you still care about him."

She could barely swallow around the aching in her chest and throat. "Of course I care about him."

"Then tell him that. Quinn is a strong confident athlete, but he's also a man. He needs to know he matters to you."

Instead of driving home, Charity got on Highway 89 and headed south, taking the exit for the Gallagher Tree Farm. She didn't know what she would say to Quinn when she saw him, only that she had to see him. She cared about Quinn too much to let the silence continue. If he was going to reject her, he would reject her, but at least she would know and not lose any more sleep wondering.

And a little voice in her whispered he wasn't going to reject her.

That same little voice whispered that she had hurt him by doubting him.

Charity knew that lack of confidence wasn't her only weakness. She was also proud. Having grown up in such humble circumstances, she was overly sensitive to slights. But Quinn had never slighted her. Quinn had never been anything but lovely.

She was nervous as she pulled into the lot, parking amidst the other half dozen vehicles.

The barn blazed with light. Fire crackled in the fire pit. Festive Christmas carols filled the frigid night air.

It took her a while to find Quinn, finally spotting him in a thicket of trees, twisting and turning a tree for a couple trying to make up their mind.

She stood back and watched him. He was smiling and joking with the couple, and so very patient as they asked him to turn the tree around again.

She felt a pang as he laughed at something the woman said because she had missed his laugh, and she had missed his smile.

She missed him.

Charity went to the barn for a cup of hot cocoa to wait for the crowd to thin so she could approach Quinn. She was in the barn studying the ornaments when Quinn and Noel walked in. Noel dashed up to her and Quinn followed more slowly.

She gave the dog a pat and then smiled nervously at Quinn. "Hi," she said.

"Noel didn't realize you were here," Quinn said.

"That's okay," she said, suddenly thinking this might not have been a good idea. Quinn didn't look happy to see her.

"It's pretty busy out there," he added.

"I saw that. Go do what you have to do. I'm happy to wait."

His eyebrow lifted.

She gave him another smile, even less steady than the one before. "Unless you don't want me to?"

"You're here for Noel."

"And you," she answered, swallowing hard. "Mostly you." She drew a quick breath. "Actually 99% you."

"I thought you were very attached to the dog."

"I am." Her heart was thumping hard. Her stomach did flips. "But I'm more attached to you. *A lot more,*" she added with emphasis.

"Hmmm."

She gestured around the barn interior. "So I'll just be here browsing and drinking cocoa until you have time to chat."

"It might be a while."

"That's okay."

He returned twenty minutes later. "It's slowing down," he said, taking a seat on the bench inside the barn. "So, let's talk while we can."

"I'm sorry," she said bluntly, certain they'd be interrupted any minute. "I'm sorry I've hurt you and sorry I didn't believe you. I'm just sorry for not being a better... friend."

"What changed your mind?" he asked.

She noticed that his easy smile was gone and his expression was guarded. The Quinn she'd met at Little Teton Resort seemed to have disappeared. Had she done that to him? To them? Her heart ached a little more. "Lots of things. Including a lot of people trying to talk sense into me."

"Like who?"

"Amanda. McKenna. Tyler. Greg."

"*Greg?*"

"I know. It was weird."

"I guess it does take a village."

She shot him a glance from beneath her lashes. "The point is, they all essentially said the same thing. That if I cared for you, then I needed to fight for you."

"So this is it? Your battle plan? You are right now fighting for me?"

"You don't need to sound scornful. I'm here and that's a big first step."

"I'm not scornful. We both know that you're really here for the dog."

"Why do you keep saying that? I'm not. I'm here because I've missed you. Terribly."

Her eyes stung and her throat thickened. "I'm crazy about you, Quinn. I want so many things with you that it scares the heck out of me. And the fact that you know all the bad things about me doesn't help me feel more secure. I told you everything in Wyoming. I told you I was a coward and insecure, but you either didn't listen or didn't believe me, which is maybe why we're in this situation now."

"So it's my fault?"

She started to protest when she realized he just might be teasing her. Her anger dissipated. "Quinn, I really am sorry. I wish I hadn't been so rattled by meeting Alice—"

"Listen, Alice scares even me. I'm sorry I wasn't there when she arrived at my house. I would have dealt with her in a way that reassured you she isn't a threat. She was part of my past, Charity, but she's not part of my future."

"Your life in Seattle makes me nervous."

"I know that."

"And you're really good-looking and I'm sure women are all over you."

"They like me," he agreed.

"So this makes you… scary."

"I'm scary?"

She wrinkled her nose. "No, you're not scary. My feelings are, though."

"Why?"

"Because I really, really like you. And I really, really don't want to lose you."

"I'm not going anywhere."

"You'll go back to Seattle soon."

"Not soon, but eventually, yes."

The weight in her chest was back. "And then you'd forget me. Not intentionally, of course—"

"Hard to forget you, sweetheart, if you're in Seattle with me."

Her heart skipped and her eyes widened and she couldn't find words, because going to Seattle had never truly crossed her mind. She hadn't allowed herself to go there. "I don't know what to say."

"Good. Because, honestly, I don't want to discuss Seattle or baseball or any of that right now, because that's all down the road, and all of that won't matter if we're not good now." He reached out to her, hand up. "Come here, sit with me."

She let herself be pulled down onto his leg. His arms went around her, and for a moment she sat there, in the circle of his arms.

She could tell there was more on his mind, and she was reminded of what Alice had said. That he projected to people what he thought they wanted, and needed, from him. Was that true? Was Quinn not himself with her?

She covered his hands with one of hers. "Alice said—" She broke off, hating herself for mentioning Alice but needing to understand. "She said you're better in Seattle. That in Seattle you can escape the pain of this place. Is that true? Is it hard for you being here?"

He caught her fingers between two of his. "It can be."

She drew a breath and exhaled, feeling a strong pinch in her chest, near her ribs. "Do you feel like you can't be yourself when you're here?"

He didn't answer right away, and then when he did, he spoke carefully. "I don't want people worrying about me. They did enough of that when I was a boy. When I come back, I want people to be happy. It's important the people I care about are happy. Life is short. Love matters. Happiness matters."

The pinch in her chest seemed to grow and rise, pushing up into her throat and jaw, all the way to her eyes. She blinked, holding back tears. "I've been a bad friend to you," she whispered. "I forgot about us being a team. I was just thinking about me."

He squeezed her fingers. "It happens."

"You shouldn't have to carry the team, though."

His arms wrapped tighter, drawing her closer. His cheek grazed the top of her head. "It's what I do best, babe."

For some reason that nearly undid her. She struggled to keep her voice steady, "But wouldn't it be nice to know that I could carry the team if I had to?"

"I already know you can. You're a lot stronger than you give yourself credit for." He dropped a kiss on the top of her head. "You're here, aren't you?"

She didn't answer, just so very happy to sit there in the warmth of his arms. She'd missed this, being with him, feeling safe, and secure. "I need you to know something," she said after a moment. "That no matter what happens with us—"

"Don't say that."

She turned in his arms to look up into his face. "No matter what happens, you should know that I love you." Her lips quivered and she nodded, holding in emotion that threatened to burst free. "You are one of the best people I've ever known, and I'm just lucky to have met you."

"It's not luck, sweetheart," he answered. "It's fate."

"Fate?"

"Yep." He kissed the tip of her nose and then her lips. "You were meant to be with me."

Chapter Twelve

I N THE END, there was no time to make herself a spectacular dress, not when Sam needed her to work late Friday
and then Quinn was slammed at the tree farm and texted her
that they could use her at the cash register in the barn if she
didn't mind helping, and of course, she didn't mind helping.

Saturday morning she went through her fabrics and
sketches and realized that she didn't have what she needed to
make herself the dress she'd wanted, and rather than rush
things, she'd relax and wear the pale pink bridesmaid dress
she'd worn for Mandy's June wedding. With her hair pinned
up and her makeup on, she'd look pretty and elegant and no
one would even know it was recycled from Mandy's wedding.

At noon, Charity headed over to the Graff with all the
decorations for the Gallaghers' tree. The tree itself would be
waiting for her in the ballroom already anchored safely in its
stand.

Decorating took longer than she anticipated simply because she was on the event committee and there were lots of
questions that kept popping up, which required her to get off

her ladder and make calls and talk to other committee members. At the same time, it was rewarding being there as the trees were decorated and the tables were set and gradually the historic ballroom was transformed into a glittering winter wonderland.

In between fielding calls and helping make quick decisions, Charity was up and down the ladder adjacent to her eight-foot tree, wrapping the strings of miniature baseball lights around the branches, and then hanging each of the two dozen red- and blue-colored balls, before adding the silver and gold stars, and then finally, each of the signed cards in their plastic sleeves. She had twelve other special "ornaments," too, like the three bobble heads, four small navy helmets bearing Quinn's number that had been giveaways at the stadium over the years, and adorable miniature baseball bats. She added wide red wired ribbon through the tree boughs before topping the tree with Quinn's signed glove and ball. Around the base went the tree skirt made of pennants and red velvet pieces.

Charity stepped back after she'd finished everything and studied it hard, being as hard and critical as possible, and then she grinned. It looked amazing. It really did. She'd made the right decision focusing on the tree and the gala as this baseball-themed tree mattered far more to Quinn and the community than whatever she'd wear tonight.

Charity returned the ladder to the hotel staff, said goodbye to Sadie who was just finishing her tree, and drove home to shower and change because Quinn would be picking her up in less than two hours.

Amanda was at their family home when Charity arrived.

"What are you doing here?" Charity asked, as Amanda followed her into their old bedroom and closed the door. "Was there a problem with your dress? Is there something up with Mom and Dad? What's going on?"

"Nothing is going on."

"Then why are you here?"

"I'm not allowed to come home anymore?" Amanda asked sitting down on the side of the bed.

"Yes, but the timing is highly suspect." Charity chewed on her lip. "Don't tell me Alice is back—"

"She's not. *Relax.*"

"Then why aren't you home getting ready?"

"Because I've come to do your hair."

"My hair?"

"I'm a hair stylist. That's what I do for a living."

"Very funny, ha-ha."

"I'm considered one of the best in all of Crawford County."

"I've been calm all day, but now I'm about to lose my mind."

"Don't. Because I'm here to get you ready for the party." Amanda rose and went to the closet. "I'm not exactly a fairy godmother, but consider me the next best thing." She pulled a garment bag from the closet. The silvery-gray garment bag was from an exclusive Seattle department store. "Quinn was worried that with everything going on you hadn't made yourself anything to wear tonight, and so he picked out something for you just in case. He had it sent to me to keep it a surprise. I approve of his choice, by the way. I think it's very glam, very beautiful, and very *you*."

"When did he do this?"

"Tuesday or Wednesday, I think."

"While we were having that big fight?"

"I don't think he was having a big fight," Amanda answered. "I think you were fighting with yourself and then you figured out that pride is stupid and fear is even stupider—"

"I don't think that's a word."

"Stupider most definitely is. Because you were there, but you saved yourself, returning from that tortured, dark place you go when you're afraid, so that you could wear *this*." Amanda unzipped the garment bag and drew out a long black semi-sheer lace dress featuring black sequin florals. She gave it a little dance on the hanger, her smile smug. "If this isn't a Charity Wright dress, I don't know what is. Boat neckline. Long sheer lace sleeves. Lovely mermaid silhouette. Heaven!"

Goose bumps covered Charity's arms, matching the prickle sensation at her nape. "I know that designer," she whispered. "I've studied that dress a dozen times this winter."

"I'm sure you have. You've always been an Oscar de la Renta fan."

"Is it really an Oscar de la Renta gown?"

"It is, and I wasn't part of this. He picked this out for you all on his own, and do you know what I love? Nothing could be more perfect for you. This is you... beautiful, delicate, feminine, with just a hint of dark romance."

"I can't—"

"Of course you can. You absolutely can. Besides, it's a gift, and it would be hurtful to refuse his gift, especially when he's gone to such an effort to make you feel special."

"Do you know how much this dress cost? Thousands and thousands—"

"Ten thousand," Amanda said promptly. "But if that man can build a four- or five-million-dollar house overlooking Yellowstone River and only visit it a half dozen times in five years, he can afford to buy you Oscar de La Renta's entire spring collection."

"The point is, I don't need anything this expensive. I don't need his money. I just want him. I like him—no, I love him—for *him*. I love his arms and his smile and his blue eyes. I love the way he looks at me and the way he teases me, and—"

"Now you're just gushing. Please, get in the shower so I can help you dress and do your hair or I'll never get to the Graff on time, and I'm determined to be there to see you make your grand entrance."

Charity's lips twitched. "This isn't a Regency novel. There is no grand entrance."

"There will be when I'm finished with you."

AN HOUR LATER, Amanda was gone and Charity was sitting in the living room, making polite conversation with her parents as if she wasn't wearing the most beautiful dress she'd ever seen in her life. The dress fit her like a glove, and her hair was a gleaming, golden waterfall, with delicate layers framing her face, and soft waves tumbling down her back. Amanda had given her a slight sexy bump at the crown which had required a handful of pins but still managed to look natural and romantic.

Charity loved her dress, and she loved her hair, and most of all, when Quinn arrived and she opened the door, she loved the way he looked at her.

His blue gaze warmed and his lips curved and she felt a ripple of pleasure because she could see the approval in his eyes. He leaned toward her and kissed her cheek. "You look so beautiful," he whispered in her ear.

"Thank you," she answered, cheeks warming, pulse humming as she breathed in the scent of his cologne. He smelled delicious, and he looked incredibly handsome in his black dinner jacket. "I love my dress," she said. "I really do."

"First it's the dog, then it's the dress. When will it be my turn?" he teased.

"I think I already told you how I feel about you," she answered, cheeks still hot. "Now come meet my parents. They've tidied up for you, and Dad has even muted the TV."

"They didn't have to do that," he protested.

"No, they did." She slipped her arm through his and walked him from the door to the small living room, fighting yet another wave of nerves. Charity hadn't introduced her parents to any of her dates or boyfriends, not since her relationship with Joe Wyatt. "Mom, Dad, this is Quinn Douglas. Quinn, these are my parents, Tom and Julie Wright."

For the next ten minutes they made polite conversation before Charity went to get her coat and black velvet evening bag.

As they stepped outside, Charity shuddered at the blast of icy wind. "I think we're going to get more snow," she said.

"It's in the forecast," he agreed. "Looks like it'll be a white Christmas."

And then she spotted the car outside, and it wasn't his black rental truck. It was a shiny burgundy-red Range Rover. "What happened to your truck?" she asked.

"That's the problem. It wasn't my truck." He opened the passenger door for her. "So I turned it in and had my favorite car dealer deliver a car."

"I thought you had a very busy day at the tree farm."

"I did. The car dealer drove the car to me at the Gallaghers and picked up the truck and here we are."

"And Noel?"

"He's hanging tonight with Jenna and Sawyer."

"No. I meant, you don't mind driving Noel around in this brand-new car? It's a really fancy car."

"Of course not. It's an SUV. It's made for dogs and kids." He gave her a crooked smile before shutting her door and going around to the driver side. He glanced at her again as he started the car and pulled away from the curb. "You do want kids, don't you?"

"Yes."

"How many?"

"I always thought I'd love three or four."

"Do you care if they're boys or girls?"

"No. But honestly, having only had sisters, I don't know if I could raise a boy."

"You'd be an amazing mom to boys. They'd love you to death." He shifted. "And where do you want to raise your kids?"

"Marietta, of course."

"Not Paradise Valley?"

She shot him a swift look. "I probably could. If I wasn't up on a ranch high in the mountains."

"My house is by the river."

"Your house is very nice."

"Could you live there?" he persisted, slowing at the railroad tracks.

She shot him another side glance, feeling somewhat dazed and fizzy, as if she'd just swallowed a carbonated drink too fast and all the bubbles were rising up at the same time. "It depends," she said thoughtfully. "Would *you* be there?"

He laughed and his laugh sent a rush of heat and pleasure through her.

"Would you *want* me to be there?" he asked as he turned into the hotel for valet parking.

She gave a little nod. "I think so."

"You think so?"

"Well, there are still other things to be discussed."

"Such as?"

"Would we have another dog? Would we get a puppy?"

"A puppy?"

"You said this car was for dogs and kids. Plural. I just wanted to make sure you really meant dogs, plural."

"I thought you loved Noel."

"I do, but I think Noel gets lonely. Maybe Noel wouldn't take off on his long walks if he had a playmate at home."

He laughed, and the sound was so warm and rich and sexy. *He* was sexy. But he was more than sexy. Quinn was smart and loyal, patient and kind. He was truly the whole package, the protective handsome alpha male, who wanted babies and children.

She shouldn't be thinking babies already but he'd brought the topic up, and Charity wanted everything he'd mentioned in the car. She wanted to marry and have kids. She wanted to raise a family with him. She wanted to experience life with him.

And then as the valet attendant opened her door, she glanced at Quinn before stepping out of the car, and her heart did another double beat. She really shouldn't be so shallow, but tonight Quinn looked breathtaking. His elegant black coat emphasized his powerful shoulders and the crisp white shirt set off his handsome face. And because she knew in her heart that she wasn't completely shallow, she allowed herself another glance as he came around to join her to admire his piercing blue eyes and his lovely firm mouth that could kiss like nobody's business.

"You can't stop smiling," he said, taking her hand in his.

The feel of his hand against hers was delicious and electric. "I know. I'm too happy. It's a problem."

He lifted their joined hands to his mouth, pressing a warm kiss to the back of hers. "That's not a problem," he murmured. "That's a gift."

QUINN'S BASEBALL-THEMED TREE was the next to last to be auctioned off, and the bidding was fierce, with the tree's price just going up and up, before finally going for a staggering amount of money to a sports collector who wasn't even attending the gala, but had someone on the phone bidding for him. Charity was thrilled that the tree raised so much money and Quinn seemed very pleased, too. The moment the bidding ended, Charity texted Jenna to tell her that Mr. Gallagher's card collection was going to a good home, and that his collection had raised a great deal of money for the community.

After the auction portion of the evening was over, tables were shifted, revealing the dance floor. Quinn and Charity danced for the next hour and a half, helping close the party out.

"My feet are killing me," Charity said as they collected their coats from the cloak room, and then slowly walked through the lobby of the Graff with its columns and dark rich wood paneling and magnificent Christmas tree.

"I hope you had a good night," Quinn said to her after handing his ticket to the valet attendant.

"I had an amazing night," she answered. "This was such a treat. And my dress—"

"Was lucky to be worn by you," he said, cutting her words off before kissing her. "You were by far the most gorgeous woman in the room."

"You didn't see Amanda then."

"She's pretty, but you're the one I want. You're the only one I want." He held her close as the front door of the hotel opened and a blast of frigid air caught at their clothes. "Sweetheart, I don't think you understand that I have never felt this way about anyone. *Ever.* I knew you were the one right away. Even as we sat in those folding chairs at Little

Teton discussing our exes, I was counting my blessings, grateful you were single, and silently thanking Greg for being such a world class idiot that he let you go."

Her lips twitched. "You didn't."

"I did."

Headlights flashed and Quinn's burgundy car pulled up in front of the hotel. Quinn opened the door and walked Charity down the front steps, mindful of patches of ice. He slipped a folded note into the valet's hand before closing the door behind Charity.

As he settled behind the steering wheel he said, "I'm thinking of having a little party next Sunday. It would be a casual late afternoon event. I'd want you there with me, cohosting the party."

She checked her surprise because as far as she knew Quinn had never had anyone over to his house. "How many people are you thinking of inviting?"

He shrugged as he shifted into drive. "Everyone?"

"I thought you said a little party."

"It'd be very informal, like an open house. People could just drop by if it was convenient, and if not, that's fine. I'd get it catered and hire bartenders. You wouldn't have to do anything but be there with me."

Her silence must have worried him. "You don't think it's a good idea," he said after a moment.

"I just know you've been working so hard at the Gallagher's. A party like that sounds like a lot of work."

"It will be some work. Maybe a lot of work. But it seems like it's a good time to do this, and truthfully, the party is long overdue. It's my way of giving back, and maybe a way to show the community that I've come home."

CHARITY DIDN'T QUITE know what to do with herself now that the Mistletoe and Montana tree auction was over. There were no ornaments to make, no gowns to sew. All she had to do was wrap up her Christmas shopping and that seemed far less interesting than spending her evenings at the Gallaghers, helping out with the cash register or just hanging out by the fire with Noel, keeping an eye on Quinn.

During a break on Wednesday she asked him about the looming holiday party he was hosting. She'd helped him last Sunday send out evites to people and she could see from the online site the positive RSVPs kept coming in. Nearly everyone invited was responding with an enthusiastic yes. "You're going to have a big turnout," she said.

"I know. I'm glad," he said.

"Do you want me to come over and do some decorating to help you get ready for the party?"

Quinn seemed almost embarrassed. "Most of the decorating has been done. I didn't have ornaments for a tree, or any of the things needed to make it look festive, so I hired Sadie to handle putting up a tree in the great room and then give the downstairs some Christmas cheer. I hope you don't mind."

"Why would I mind? Sadie has such a great eye and so much style."

"But so do you."

"I appreciate the vote of confidence, but I prefer fashion to interior design, and just doing the baseball tree for the Mistletoe and Montana gala satisfied my tree decorating itch for the year. This Christmas tree stuff is a lot of work." She rubbed her hands together before the fire. "What about food? You've got that all sorted, too?"

"Flintworks is catering, and sending over a bartender. Copper Mountain Gingerbread and Dessert Factory is doing desserts. Risa is doing flowers. I even have some kids from the high school's chorale dropping by to sing some carols."

"You've thought of everything."

"Have I?" He rubbed the back of his neck. "I feel like I'm forgetting something."

"If it comes to you, let me know and I'll handle it for you. But otherwise, don't worry. You're going to have a great turnout and everyone will have fun."

CHARITY WAS RIGHT, Quinn thought, moving through the crowded great room to add another log to the fire.

People kept arriving and no one seemed inclined to leave. Most of those that came early weren't people from Marietta, either, but Paradise Valley neighbors, and not his neighbors now—most of those who'd built custom homes in his area were a mix of celebrities and affluent people from the East and West Coasts that wanted a piece of Montana wilderness to add to their collection of vacation homes—but the folks Quinn had known growing up.

All the Sheenans came, not completely a surprise since Trey had married his sister, but it meant a lot to Quinn to have five of the six brothers in his house, with their wives and children. The Carrigan sisters came, too, as they had been close neighbors and Beverly Carrigan had always been kind to Quinn's mother. Sage brought chocolates which pleased Charity to no end. The MacCreadies attended, as well as bull rider Chase Garrett, who'd bought the Douglas ranch from Rory a year ago. There were a dozen other prominent ranching families in attendance and Quinn made time to greet every single one of them.

He was beyond grateful as the Flint brothers arrived, and then the Scott brothers arrived, and the Vaughns from the Bar V5 Ranch. Charity's sister, Amanda, and her husband Tyler were one of the first to come and last to leave. At one point there were so many people in his house that it reminded him of a nightclub at midnight, but Quinn loved it.

He looked for Charity and she was leaning against the kitchen island talking animatedly with his sister and Sage and several other women from Marietta. She was wearing a simple sweater dress and boots and yet she glowed as she laughed with the others. She was never more beautiful than when she was happy, and he'd do everything in his power to make her happy.

His gaze shifted to the big hearth which crackled and popped with a log fire. To the right of the fire was Rusty Noel dozing in his new red plaid dog bed, his eye opening now and then to keep watch, before going back to sleep.

Quinn felt a rush of gratitude as he took it all in. His neighbors and friends. His family. His love and their good-boy dog.

He loved how his house could hold everyone, and with the holiday decorations up, it looked amazing. Best of all, it felt amazing. His big sprawling house had finally become his home.

CHARITY SAW QUINN step out the back door at one point during the party to take a call. When he returned he had an odd look on his face, one she couldn't quite decipher. She made her way through the crowd to go to his side. "Is everything all right?" she asked, putting a hand on his back.

He nodded and wrapped his arm around her. "Everything is good," he answered, giving her a hug.

"I'm glad."

And yet as the afternoon continued, she thought Quinn seemed preoccupied in a way he hadn't been earlier.

What had the call been about? Was it Alice phoning? Or was it something else?

There was still so much about Quinn that she didn't know. She had strong feelings for him, and this sizzling physical attraction, but they were still two people with separate lives. Separate lives weren't necessarily a bad thing, but she wondered how they would navigate their relationship once he returned to Seattle. From what she'd heard others say, baseball went on for months. When Quinn left for spring training, he wouldn't be back until September or October. The idea of being apart for nine months was beyond daunting. It was too long. She didn't want to do it, and yet how could she go to Seattle on her own?

Finally at seven, the house was empty. Charity had stood next to Quinn at the door while he thanked the last of his guests for coming today and wishing them merry Christmas as they left. Now she sat on the couch and watched Quinn move around the room and check on candles that had burned low and add another log to the fire.

"That was a lovely party," she said, reaching for the soft cashmere blanket draped artfully over the arm of the leather couch. "And you, Mr. Douglas, were an excellent host."

"Can I get you anything to drink?" he asked.

"No, I'm perfect. Thank you. Grab something for yourself if you want."

"I'm good, too," he said, sitting next to her, his arm going around her shoulders. He kissed her on her forehead. "Thank you for being here."

"My pleasure. I wouldn't have wanted to be anywhere

but here with you." She hesitated a moment, wondering how to mention what had been on her mind ever since he'd taken that call earlier. "I am a little worried about something, and since we're teammates, I'm going to just ask."

"Sounds like a smart plan."

"You had a call during the party, right about halfway through, and you stepped outside the kitchen door, but when you returned, you seemed upset. You said everything was good but something in that call changed your mood."

Quinn didn't answer right away. He stared across the room to the big tree covered in vintage glass ornaments. "It was terrible timing," he said at length. "It still is."

"What happened?"

He drew a slow breath. "Rusty Noel's owners have decided they want him back."

"*What?*" She scrambled into a taller sitting position, and shifted to better see his face.

"They say their son is heartbroken. They tried to get him a puppy but he doesn't want the puppy. He wants his dog back—"

"But that family doesn't take care of Noel! They haven't even tried to see him all this time."

"That was the parents' decision, not the boy's, and they've realized they made a mistake."

"Too bad. Too late. You can't just abandon a dog and then take him back."

"They're coming tonight to pick Rusty up."

"*No!* No. Quinn, no. Tell me you're not going to let them do that."

"Rusty is legally their dog."

"Call Dr. Sullivan. He can vouch for us. He knows the situation. He was the one who told us those owners have given up."

"I talked to Noah, today, when he was at the party. He'd talked to the owners already. That's how they had my number. He passed it on to them."

"And Dr. Sullivan thinks they should just get Noel back?" She turned to look at Noel who was watching them, head cocked, clearly paying attention, because that was the kind of dog he was. Loyal and loving and attentive. Her eyes watered and she sniffled. "His owners are terrible people. They don't deserve him. Noel is the best dog I've ever met. He deserves a home where he's going to be cherished, and loved. Quinn, he belongs with us."

"But, sweetheart, he's not ours."

She jumped off the couch, and crossed to the fire to sit down next to Noel. She buried her face in his silky coat and fought tears, but it was a losing battle. Quinn let her cry, too. When she lifted her head long minutes later, she looked at him, tears streaking her face. "When are they coming?"

"They'll be here in an hour."

THEY ARRIVED IN less than an hour. Charity didn't know if

it was a good or bad thing that they arrived so quickly. She was just so upset. She hadn't seen this coming.

When the family pulled up, she'd expected to dislike them on sight, and she tried to dislike them, but when their little boy, an eight-year-old with shaggy blond hair and a huge smile, tumbled from the car and ran straight to Rusty to throw his arms around the dog, Charity felt the sting of tears in her eyes.

The boy was so happy to see his dog, and it wasn't a one-sided affection. Rusty whined and smothered the boy with licks and kisses, his tail wagging frantically. He practically crawled into the boy's lap and they rolled around on the floor, delighted to be together. It was a love affair, she thought, and as much as she wanted to be mad at his family, she couldn't be upset with the little boy who clearly loved his dog.

Thankfully, it was Quinn who made polite conversation with the parents. The mother and father looked awkward as they spoke with him, but then they turned to Charity and thanked her for taking such good care of Rusty. "We know you were the one that rescued him. Thank you. We appreciate it. We do as we know from Dr. Sullivan that you've grown attached to him."

Charity struggled to smile. It was incredibly difficult. "I'm just glad your son will have his dog for Christmas."

A few more minutes of awkward conversation followed and then they excused themselves, taking Rusty. Rusty only hesitated once, standing on the doorstep glancing from Quinn to Charity and back again before following the boy out into the car where he lay down in the back seat, his head on the boy's leg.

Blinking back tears, Charity scooped up Rusty Noel's new Christmas plaid dog bed and the pottery water bowl she'd bought him that featured dogs wearing garlands and jaunty red bows, and carried it all out to the car. "These are his," she said. "He should have them."

It had begun to snow earlier, Charity didn't even know the moment it began, but as they loaded up the car, the fat snowflakes fell thickly, quickly covering the roof of the car and the trees and the front yard. The father brushed the white flakes from the red plaid bed, emptied the water bowl, and put both in the trunk. Quinn gave Rusty a scratch goodbye, and then Charity reached into the car and gave Rusty Noel one last pat, before stepping back.

Quinn put his arm around her and together they watched the car go, disappearing into the falling snow.

Inside the house she cried against his chest, absolutely worn out. The last few weeks had been hectic, filled with activity and so many emotions, and it all hit her hard. The tears fell for a little bit and then Charity pulled herself together and reached for a tissue to wipe her cheeks and blow her nose. "Okay, that was hard," she said. "I didn't dream when I woke up this morning that I'd be saying goodbye to Noel tonight."

"It was hard, and unexpected," Quinn agreed.

She nodded sadly and scrubbed her face dry with one more tissue. "I really didn't see it coming."

"It's not the way today was supposed to end."

She managed a watery smile. "It's definitely not fair to you, Quinn. You threw a fantastic party. You were an incredible host. Your house looked gorgeous. You should be proud of yourself."

"Thank you." He lightly rubbed her back. "Are you going to be okay?"

Charity drew a deep breath, trying to regroup. "I will be," she said, and it was true. Part of her was happy for Rusty Noel. He was back with his boy, whom he clearly loved. And if this was what was best for the dog and child, she should be happy for them. It would be selfish of her to keep the beautiful retriever when he had somewhere he belonged. "But it's been such a roller coaster this December, and Christmas isn't even here yet."

"Just two more days," Quinn said, drawing her toward the Christmas tree. "But not too early for you to find your ornament."

"I have an ornament?"

"You do, indeed. You'll know it's yours because it has your name on it."

"Where is it?" she asked, facing the huge tree. It was easily fourteen feet tall and covered with countless glass ornaments. Her brows pulled as she studied the gorgeous tree shimmering with light. "You need to give me a little hint."

"It's not too high and not too low," he said.

"That doesn't help much," she grumbled. "You're considerably taller than me." She tucked her hair behind her ears and kept searching. "Give me another hint. What color is the ornament?"

"Silver, I think," he said stepping back to give her space. "Well, maybe gold. But it has your name on it, and a little sparkly red ribbon." He went to the couch, and moved some of the pillows around, and then dropped into one of the leather armchairs facing the tree. "Warm," he said, as she moved a branch, and then another. "Warmer," he added as she studied an ornament. "Ah, hot. Hotter." He stopped talking and simply watched as she reached for a silver-gold ball with a bit of calligraphy that read Charity.

She unhooked the hanger and turned around with the ornament in her hands and blinked as she looked at Quinn, and then the red silk pillows on the couch, each pillow a letter that spelled out *marry me*.

"Quinn?" she whispered, shocked.

"Open your ornament," he said.

Hands trembling, she carefully lifted the top of the ornament and inside was a stunning diamond ring. She couldn't move, she couldn't think, she couldn't breathe.

Her head jerked up as Quinn went down on one knee.

Was this really happening?

"Charity, I love you, and I know it's been a rough day,

but I'm not going anywhere, not today, not tomorrow, not ever. Marry me. I want you in my life forever."

"Teammates," she said, unable to hide her smile.

"For life," he said, extending his hand to her. "What do you say?"

Tears filled her eyes as she put her hand into his. "Absolutely, 100% yes."

CHAPTER THIRTEEN

I T WAS A stunning ring, with a huge diamond. She had never seen anything so big, or sparkly, or stunning.

Charity didn't remember putting the ring on her finger, and maybe she didn't. Maybe Quinn took the ring from the box and put it on her finger, but suddenly it was there, and she lifted her hand, holding the ring to the light, turning her finger this way and that just to see the diamond sparkle and glow with an inner blue fire. It was extraordinary. The proposal was extraordinary.

"Is this really happening?" she asked huskily.

"It absolutely is," he answered firmly. "I spent the past twenty-eight days trying to figure out how to make you mine. It hasn't been easy. You were determined to remain single."

"People will think we're crazy getting engaged after just a few weeks."

"Those people don't know you, and they don't know me."

"And I don't think they know we're meant to be a team."

"I couldn't have said that better. We are meant to be together. It wasn't until I met you that I realized the reason I was still single was that I hadn't met *you* yet. Once I met you, game over. I'd found my woman. You are my other half, Charity. You are my heart. Everything I am, everything I have, is yours—"

"I want you, not your things. In fact, you could have nothing and I would love you just as much… maybe even more."

"I know you're not interested in my money, but that doesn't mean I don't want to provide for you, and take care of you, just as I want to take care of our kids, and our families. It's why I work so hard, so I can provide."

"I'm not used to being spoiled, and I can't get over this ring." She extended her fingers, dazzled by the sparkling diamond. "Oh, it's really lovely. When did you get it?"

"I drove to Bozeman earlier in the week and looked at rings."

"So this is from Bozeman."

"No, it's actually from a jeweler in San Francisco. I didn't like what I saw in Bozeman and so my jeweler flew out a selection of rings for me yesterday and I liked this one best. The oval cut is classic, but the diamond has so much fire, and the fire reminded me of you."

"It has a lot of fire because it's a *huge* diamond, Quinn."

"The better to defend yourself in a barroom fight."

She couldn't stifle her giggle. "I have never been in a barroom fight."

"I'm just saying."

She leaned toward him, and kissed him, and then kissed him again. "I love it. And you. So very, very much."

He shifted one of the scarlet silk *M* pillows from behind his back and tossed it onto a chair across from him. His gaze swept the room, lingering on the fireplace. "One day we'll have little stockings hanging from that mantel."

"And toys under the tree," she added, snuggling closer, relishing the feel of his arm around her. His strength made her feel so secure. "I can't wait until we have a family. Does that scare you?"

"Not at all."

"Seriously? Because I'd love for us to have a baby on the way this time next year, or maybe even a baby," she said hopefully, looking up at him. "Is that too soon for you?"

"I'm a family man. I want kids. That's why I built a big house."

"And bought a car for kids and dogs," she added with a grin.

He kissed the top of her head. "You will be an amazing mom. I just hope I can be as good a dad."

"You will. You absolutely will, and when we have hard times, we will help each other. We'll be a strong team, you and me."

Emotion shadowed his face, darkening his eyes. A small muscle pulled in his jaw. It took him a moment to speak. "My parents were proud of being a team. Even when they had differences of opinions they tried to find a way to come together. That is so important to me."

He brushed a long tendril of hair back from her cheek. "You are so important to me. I don't think you have any idea of just how much I love you, and need you. I do need you, too. You're my person, my other half. I've been missing you all these years."

"And here I was in Marietta—" She broke off, wrinkled her nose. "Actually, I was in Wyoming."

He laughed, and clasped her face, kissing her breathless. The kiss lasted a very long time.

It was much, much later when he lifted his head and pushed back a wave of gleaming hair from her face. "Do you have any thoughts on the wedding? Should we wait until after this next season ends—"

"No. Because how would we have a Christmas baby if we're not even going to get married until next fall?"

"So you want to marry before spring training?"

"Can we?"

"That would mean a late January or early February wedding."

"We can do that, can't we? As I'd rather go to Seattle as your wife than just some crazy fan in the stands."

His grinned ruefully. "You don't have to worry about groupies. I'm not interested in them. I never have been. I shouldn't have even mentioned it."

"I'm glad you did. It's better to be prepared."

"This baseball career might be hard on you. There are long weeks where I'll be on the road."

"Then I'll use that time to work on my designs, and maybe come home and catch up with everyone." She hesitated. "If we can afford the plane tickets."

"We can."

"Good, then that's what I'll do." She sat back and thought for another moment. "Where do you want to get married?"

"I'd think you'd want to marry in Marietta. Maybe St. James?"

"No, not necessarily." She chewed her lip. "I was thinking maybe we should do a destination wedding. Marry where this whole thing started." She gave him a hopeful look. "How about a winter wedding at Little Teton? That way most of our family could drive there and they could ice-skate and ski and I'm sure your friend Peter would welcome the business."

"And your friend Tricia Thorpe could actually see the resort for herself."

"You invite some of your major league player friends and they can see the resort and tell their friends, and maybe even a real sportswriter will go and write about it in a national paper or magazine."

He started to laugh. "Wait a minute. Is this all a ploy just to help out the resort?"

"It *is* a very nice resort."

"It is," he agreed, brushing a kiss across her lips.

"And it is where we met," she added.

"I love the idea," he answered, kissing her again before drawing her against his chest. "And I love you even more for wanting to help out Peter. You have a huge heart, Charity Wright. I love your beautiful heart so very much."

"And it all belongs to you," she murmured, happy, so happy just to be in the circle of Quinn's arms and feel the magic and wonder of his love. It was truly the most amazing thing.

Quinn Douglas loved her. He loved *her*, Charity Wright, the woman who had almost given up on her happy-ever-after. And just when she didn't think she could hang in there any longer, Quinn appeared, stronger, smarter, and braver than any romance hero she'd ever read in any of her books.

"I love you," she whispered lifting her head to smile up at him, tears stinging her eyes. She reached up to lightly touch his mouth. His lips were firm against her fingertips. She blinked back her happy tears as she replaced her fingers with her mouth. She kissed him gently, sweetly. "You are the best Christmas gift ever."

"I'm just glad you said yes."

"Did you even doubt it?"

"It was a very whirlwind courtship and I know you are risk averse."

"I am, but you're my safe place. I know without a doubt that you have my back."

"I do."

She was silent a moment, listening to the crackle and pop of the fire. "Because of you I'm no longer hunkered down behind my wagon. I'm out there, living again."

"Taking risks, having adventures," he said.

"Yes."

"Because I also know that we'll always be able to come back here. This is home."

He smiled. "Exactly."

"You don't really know how many years of baseball you have left, do you?"

Quinn shook his head. "There may only be one year left. Or, if I'm healthy and playing well like I did this year, there might be another couple of years in me. I don't know."

"You don't have to know. I'm going to be fine living in Seattle, or wherever you are, because where you are is where I want to be."

"I thought you couldn't stand the thought of living in Pray."

"I think I would have been happy, if Joe had been the right one for me. But he wasn't. You're the one I need. You're the one I want."

He cupped the back of her head, and drew her close to kiss her. "Now that I've found you, I can't imagine a future without you. I can't imagine happiness or family or children with anyone but you."

"Not happiness or family," she echoed, the corners of her lips lifting. "Or Christmas," she added, kissing him back. "After this, it wouldn't ever be Christmas without you."

EPILOGUE

I T ENDED UP being a huge wedding at the Little Teton Resort.

Everyone invited came, from Quinn's teammates to friends from college. All of Marietta and Paradise Valley seemed to have made the drive over the Teton Pass, too, with the exception of Sawyer and Jenna Gallagher who were home with their newborn son, but they sent love. Indeed, Quinn and Charity felt nothing but love from all their family and friends who'd traveled to Wyoming to celebrate their big day, which was really a big weekend, packed with laughter, activities, and fun.

The weather held up all weekend, with just a dusting of snow as the ceremony began in the little chapel on the outskirts of Little Teton. Charity's four bridesmaids—Jenny, Mandy, McKenna, Sadie—looked beautiful in shades of deep blue, each of them wearing a custom gown designed just for them by Charity. McKenna and Rory's little girl was the flower girl and TJ played ring bearer. Charity designed her own dress, and it was the kind of dress a romantic would wear for a winter wedding, and of course Amanda did her hair. Charity felt like a princess as she spotted Quinn at the front of the church. Quinn and his groomsmen were dashing in black tuxedos but Charity only had eyes for Quinn who took her breath away.

She loved him, profoundly.

He'd changed her world. Because of him, she had so much more confidence and she viewed the future with humor and hope.

Life was good, very good, and her glass wasn't merely half-full, but overflowing with blessings.

THE END

The Taming of the Sheenans

The Sheenans are six powerful wealthy brothers from Marietta, Montana. They are big, tough, rugged men, and as different as the Montana landscape.

Christmas at Copper Mountain
Book 1: Brock Sheenan's story

Tycoon's Kiss
Book 2: Troy Sheenan's story

The Kidnapped Christmas Bride
Book 3: Trey Sheenan's story

Taming of the Bachelor
Book 4: Dillion Sheenan's story

A Christmas Miracle for Daisy
Book 5: Cormac Sheenan's story

The Lost Sheenan's Bride
Book 6: Shane Sheenan's story

Available now at your favorite online retailer!

Want to know more about Quinn's siblings? Check out the Douglas family stories!

Miracle on Chance Avenue
Rory Douglas's story

The Kidnapped Christmas Bride
McKenna Douglas's story

Don't miss the other Wright sister stories!

Take a Chance on Me
Amanda Wright's story

Take Me, Cowboy
Jenny Wright's story

Available now at your favorite online retailer!

You've been introduced to Joe Wyatt. Look out for his story spring 2019!
Sign up for our newsletter for the latest details
tulepublishing.com/about/#subscribe

ABOUT THE AUTHOR

New York Times and USA Today bestselling author of over fifty five romances and women's fiction titles, **Jane Porter** has been a finalist for the prestigious RITA award five times and won in 2014 for Best Novella with her story, Take Me, Cowboy, from Tule Publishing. Today, Jane has over 12 million copies in print, including her wildly successful, Flirting With Forty, picked by Redbook as its Red Hot Summer Read, and reprinted six times in seven weeks before being made into a Lifetime movie starring Heather Locklear. A mother of three sons, Jane holds an MA in Writing from the University of San Francisco and makes her home in sunny San Clemente, CA with her surfer husband and two dogs.

Thank you for reading

Not Christmas Without You

If you enjoyed this book, you can find more from all our great authors at TulePublishing.com, or from your favorite online retailer.

TULE
PUBLISHING